Dedication

I dedicate this book to my close friends from high school and college. Their love of telling stories was an inspiration for me, and I sincerely appreciated their encouragement to finish this project. I won't name them all, as I will surely forget someone. Thanks again!

The Rise of the Deep State

Eric Frick

Published by Eric Frick, 2022.

This is a work of fiction. Similarities to real people, places, or events are entirely coincidental.

THE RISE OF THE DEEP STATE

First edition. January 22, 2022.

Copyright © 2022 Eric Frick.

ISBN: 979-8227689429

Written by Eric Frick.

Table of Contents

Chapter 1 Meet Jack, Lucy, and Frank

Jack Brown ate his breakfast, not yet realizing that soon, he would uncover history's most colossal conspiracy and plot against the United States. Part of Jack's routine was to get up at 5am and go for a quick run, either on his treadmill or around his suburban Georgetown neighborhood, before beginning his commute to Langley, Virginia, and CIA's headquarters.

On this day, Jack decided the weather was good enough to take his run outdoors; he preferred it, but not if it was raining heavily or too much snow was on the ground. Even with that, he usually toughened the elements.

Running was part of Jack's ecosystem, his daily ritual, and he looked forward to getting some exercise and clearing his mind. He used this time to reflect on the day's events and make the Gremlins bothering his brain about projects or problems with work colleagues disappear.

He has always felt uneasy on days where he cannot run, like something is missing. It was as though he couldn't be on an even keel the entire day unless he had his early morning run to clear out his system. Today, he didn't have the usual strain dealing with people issues, and he used the time to reflect the recent excellent progress they were having in ramping up jobs in the quantum computing lab he managed for the CIA.

Jack finished his run a little faster than usual and returned home to shower. Letting the lukewarm spray cascade over him was his last moment of peace before the busy commute to Langley. He quickly dressed and headed into the kitchen.

"Good morning, and happy Monday," said his wife, Lucy, as she frantically finished up her morning routine and got ready for work.

"A Monday it is!" Jack grumbled in response. He was not much of a morning talker and had a lot on his mind about the upcoming day and workweek.

Lucy smiled at Jack and continued, "The weather definitely picked up over the weekend, maybe warm enough to put the top down on the car."

Jack chuckled, "That's the plan; what's the point in owning a convertible you can only use a hundred days a year?"

Even under the best of circumstances, Jack's commute was at least an hour and was usually a full-time battle, with hellish traffic and terrible weather at this time of year, including snow. However, he hoped it would be peaceful today. He would get into the office a little earlier to get a heads up on his day, especially since every Monday started with the dreaded staff meeting. Jack gave Lucy a quick goodbye and jumped into his BMW 325 to begin his commute into CIA headquarters.

. . . .

Jack and Lucy were complete opposites. While Jack was more of a methodical step-by-step person, Lucy was much more of a free spirit, with the unique talent to take a complete mess and organize it quickly and effectively. This talent had landed her a job as chief of staff for Senator Graben, Ohio's senior senator.

Lucy was a political science major in college and had always dreamed of working on Capitol Hill. She had started this job about a year ago and still hadn't gotten over the feeling that she had finally achieved her dream job.

Her day started a little later than Jack's, so she took her time getting ready for her daily commute — a relatively short one since they lived in Georgetown.

On this day, she was running a little later than usual and glanced out the window to check the weather; it didn't take much for her to make an excuse to order an Uber on most days, as parking was always a hassle. The only days she preferred to drive were when she might get out early and do something. That had been a rare occurrence lately since she was working late into the evening, juggling multiple priorities for the senator.

. . . .

Jack had loaded up his backpack, complete with a snack, and took off his winter coat, folding it neatly and placing it on the car's backseat. After packing up the rest of the day's supplies, he backed out of the garage and navigated out of his neighborhood, traveling onto the major thoroughfare that would lead him down to Langley. He soon settled into his morning commute. If the traffic wasn't too heavy and there was no severe weather, Jack actually enjoyed this time; it allowed him to reflect on his projects and other important things in his life. Today, he reflected on his new assignment of being the technical lead in the CIA's quantum computing lab. This project represented a dream come true for him as it combined state-of-the-art technology and some incredible software challenges.

Jack held a Ph.D. in computer science from Wright State University just outside Dayton, Ohio. He initially built up a software development background while working as a defense contractor at Wright-Patterson Air Force Base, where he had spent years developing state-of-the-art software. Jack was a skilled software developer and an incredibly capable manager with the skills to manage and direct extensive complex software development projects.

This expertise led the CIA to hire him to lead some of their most technologically advanced IT projects, including the quantum computing lab, which was the most coveted advanced project in the agency. The CIA had selected Jack to be the technical director, an excellent opportunity for Jack and his family.

Quantum computing is an entirely innovative new technology with the promise to revolutionize information processing. Quantum computers run on a completely unique architecture than traditional and can exponentially increase computing power, potentially leaping humankind twenty years into the future. Achieving this type of processing power could revolutionize many of the world's industries and solve some of its most complex problems.

On his commute, Jack thought about the limitless possibilities of how this computing power could solve some of the world's most pressing problems. He recalled a recent pitch from a medical firm on how they could solve complex genome problems in synthesizing new incredible drugs to cure certain diseases that have plagued humanity for centuries. On this day, Jack only thought about those positive aspects of quantum computing and the remarkable breakthroughs it might provide.

Since Jack was the eternal optimist and only saw the positive side of things, he rarely considered any downside of such a revolutionary technology, like this technology falling into the wrong hands. Jack had not considered the impact of enterprising criminals using this fantastic technology. On this day, Jack merely thought about how well the initial project was going in the goal line of delivering a complete operational lab to the agency within the next six months.

．．．．

Jack only had a few minutes to grab his coffee before heading to the Monday morning staff meeting, scheduled and run by Jack's boss, Jeff Yanko. Everyone looked around with nervous tension when Jeff walked into the room, immediately taking control of the meeting.

Jack could feel the energy drain from the room as everyone's eyes seemed to gloss over; Yanko was a complete nightmare. He had a way of getting under people's skin, and particularly at the staff meeting, where he liked to single people out early Monday morning to set an example for the week. These meetings were unbearably uncomfortable for everyone involved, but the staff would all laugh about it afterward to relieve some of the tension.

By all rights, Yanko had the same credentials as Jack, with a Ph.D. in computer science and several published and respected technical papers. Jack had always felt that, deep down, Yanko really hated working with technology and far preferred playing the politics game every chance he got. Not surprising, since Jeff had risen to his position by doing this very thing at an expert level. Yanko always seemed on the warpath, never genuinely interested in the people or the tech, but just further climbing the government ladder.

He had undoubtedly gained enemies with how fast he had climbed, but then again, Jack thought, who hadn't? Still, Yanko's current staff really disliked him, and he made it easy for them to do so. They also routinely wrote off his technical opinions, not so much the facts but because of their extreme dislike for him.

The meetings usually started with routine business and ended after an hour, and this Monday was no exception. Yanko seemed rushed to get through the day's agenda; far too hurried to chew anyone out, which resonated well with the staff. It was odd, though, almost out of character.

Jack leaned back in his chair and groaned when the meeting was finally over.

"Frank," he said, "I really dread these Monday morning meetings."

Eric Frank Jr. sat across from him and replied, "I know what you mean; I just can't stand them, and I can't wait to get a doughnut and some coffee to celebrate it being over!"

. . . .

Eric Frank Jr. was a junior accountant whom the agency had hired a couple of years ago. He and Jack quickly became friends, with everybody referring to him as Frank, as he seemed to naturally go by the name.

Frank was a tall man with an athletic frame. He had played power forward as a walk-on player at the University of Dayton. At work, he had the reputation of being a tenacious employee with great attention to detail. Even though he had only been at the agency a couple of years, his coworkers had a great deal of respect for his work.

"Jack," Frank began, "we need to grab some coffee at lunch; you wouldn't believe the round I had yesterday."

Jack laughed, "Absolutely; we need to get back out there — it's been too long."

Frank smiled warmly, "You have my number; I hope you also hand over the customary hundred and get lunch after I win by five strokes."

They both chuckled and strolled down the hallway to grab a cup of coffee and talk about the day's events. Frank glanced over at Jack after pouring his cup of coffee and said, "Hey, I've got some stuff going on; I've been looking at some of these audits that I'd like you to take a look at."

"I would be happy to take a look at it. What's it about?" Jack replied.

"It's about the quantum computing lab," Frank explained. "Something just doesn't seem quite right. I'd like you to see if there's anything worthwhile looking into before I take it any further."

"Yeah, I would be happy to take a look at them," Jack answered as he sipped his coffee. "Drop the papers by my office, and I'll go through them this evening."

Frank thanked him and was happy to go about his day now that he had recharged with his doughnut and a giant cup of coffee.

Jack also took off toward his office, that day's duties in the back of his mind. He knew that Frank wanted him to look at these papers before he talked to Yanko; he didn't truly trust Jack's boss, and Jack certainly wanted to look at anything concerning the quantum computing lab before Yanko got his hands on it.

. . . .

After a long day of meetings, Jack packed up for his drive home to get ready for an evening out — dinner with Lucy at their favorite Italian restaurant. They had not had a chance to go out in a while, so he was especially looking forward to it. While on his way out of the door, Jack briefly glanced back and spotted the file Frank had given him earlier. He quickly grabbed it and stuffed it in his bag, vowing to review it after dinner.

He had no idea the information in that file would change both his life and the country's fate.

It had been a long time since Jack and Lucy had the opportunity to go out to dinner, just the two of them. They had a kind of ritual to go out at least once a week when they first moved to DC, spending some time together and blowing off a little steam.

They arrived at their favorite Italian restaurant. Thankfully this evening, there wasn't much of a crowd, so they didn't have to wait long for a table. When the host called them, the maître d' recognized them and greeted them by name, asking why they had not been in a while.

Jack replied, "We've both been so busy with work that we've had no time to go out whatsoever. Please don't think we're trying to avoid you or that there's something wrong with the service. This restaurant is far and wide our favorite place."

Without missing a step, the maître d' replied, "Good; I was beginning to worry I had lost my touch."

"No danger of that!" Jack laughed.

He and Lucy both took their seats and reviewed the menu, though only through habit, as they both picked their favorite entrees with no need for the menu at all. This was all part of the process for them to begin relaxing and enjoy the evening. They both loved this restaurant because it had a tranquil, subtle atmosphere — the complete opposite of a hectic day job.

Before ordering, Jack and Lucy selected their favorite bottle of red wine; dinner at a place like this would just not be complete without it.

Jack began the conversation. "I don't know about you, but I was really looking forward to this evening. We have not done this in such a long time; I truly miss it."

"Words cannot describe how happy I am to be at dinner here with you," Lucy smiled. "I hope this isn't permanent, where finding just a couple of hours to go out to dinner becomes an impossible task."

Jack looked at her thoughtfully. "I was thinking the same thing just the other day. We have worked so hard to get to this point, but I wonder if this is what we're really looking for."

"Well, let's not go overboard," she chuckled. "I think we can handle the situation just fine for now; we just need to work a bit harder at finding time for each other."

The mood became much lighter now that conversation was out of the way, and they discussed more routine topics and had a delightful dinner together. The time went by quickly, even though they spent hours at the restaurant. They were enjoying it so much that they simply did not want to leave.

After a brief discussion with the waiter and finishing up the bill, Jack and Lucy headed home to turn into bed early and finish their relaxing evening.

• • • •

Jack's favorite thing in the evening was to have a bit of scotch before heading to bed, just to help him sleep a little better and take the day's edge off. However, he thought against it tonight since he'd had quite a bit of wine for dinner.

For some reason, even though he and Lucy had spent all evening at dinner, Jack was still feeling a little energetic and needed to do something to wind down. He headed to his home office to browse around for something to do when he remembered the quantum computing lab file Frank had given him earlier that day.

Jack retrieved the file from his bag and began looking through the file to see what Frank had described to him. The report was a mix of operational and financial data that management pulled every month to sample the quantum lab's operation. This report was meant to be a high-level summary with supporting details.

Not many people could understand this type of report since it included operational data about the computational facility and the network and finances allocated to operate it. Jack had the technical depth along with the right financial background to digest this kind of data quickly.

Things seem to be as expected upon his first review of the report. But after taking a second pass-through, Jack saw some abnormalities with the operational data.

He discovered spikes and activity during typical downtimes for the facility, an unusual but steady increase in the amount of processing CPU the servers allocated. Government facilities typically attribute this type of spike to jobs consuming more CPU. However, the billing did not accurately reflect the CPU memory being consumed.

To make matters a little more alarming, these were not small spikes but appeared to be a regular increase in the number of jobs running in the off-hours and were simply not included in the billing. It would take more investigation, but the number of billing resources was unbalanced. It was almost as though phantom jobs were being run and not being accounted for whatsoever.

Jack thought that these reporting irregularities were nothing too distressing, but he was glad Frank had approached him about this and would follow up with him in the morning.

. . . .

The following morning, Jack headed down to the break room to grab his morning cup of coffee. Frank walked in as he poured the hot liquid into his cup.

"Hey, Frank, how are you doing this morning?"

"I'm doing okay," Frank said with a smile, "but I really need my morning cup of coffee."

"I'm hoping it will do magic with me as well," Jack replied, then quickly added, "I took a look at those audits you gave me yesterday."

This raised Frank's interest. "Well, what did you think?"

Jack's expression changed; he was serious about this and measuring his response.

"There's something very odd going on with these numbers," Jack began, "but I would like to take another pass at them this evening. I'm also not sure the break room is the right place to discuss this," he added, lowering his tone.

"I thought they were strange when I first looked at them," Frank agreed. "I couldn't make sense of it, which is why I wanted you to take a look."

Jack nodded, "Thanks for getting the data to me; I really appreciate it. I want to think about some options before any next steps. I'll get back to you shortly."

"Then, I'll wait to hear from you."

With that, both Frank and Jack headed out of the break room and back to their offices.

. . . .

Later that evening, Jack relaxed at home with his late-night scotch, thinking about the day's activities. He was suspicious about the goings-on at the quantum lab and wanted to dig further into the monthly report's anomalies.

However, he remembered his conversation with Lucy the other evening and noted how hard they had worked to get into this position. He did not want to do anything to jeopardize his dream job, and this certainly had the potential to do just that within his management structure. Jack had realized early in his position at the CIA that he had to be very careful about where he stuck his nose and what type of digging he could do into expenditures and reporting structures.

He also realized that this could be just a mere technical error and that, most probably, nothing was going on at all. Maybe he and Frank were just letting their imaginations run away with them by imagining something sinister was behind mere accounting irregularities. For the time being, Jack would file it away, sleep on it, and process it in the morning.

The following day, Jack went on his usual morning run; it was the perfect time to unwrap his thoughts from the previous evening, where Jack could press himself extremely hard in a run while trying to sort out something in his mind. It was not a particularly good morning for it, as it was raining and a little cold outside, but once Jack got started, he focused solely on the decision at hand. Should he press ahead and look into the quantum lab's problems, perhaps risking his career?

The more he ran, the more he felt like something was digging into his side — the feeling that he needed to look into this further, and there was probably something going on here. With the run cleansing his mind, Jack had a new sense of purpose and decided to schedule another meeting with Frank to talk things over.

. . . .

Jack immediately checked Frank's calendar when he got into work the following day. He set up a meeting for later that morning in Jack's office to discuss the results of the monthly quantum computing performance report and any issues Frank had spotted.

When the time came, Jack heard a knock on his door.

"Come on in, Frank," he called.

Frank opened the door, carefully closing it behind him, and made his way to one of the visitors' chairs in front of Jack's desk.

Jack opened up by thanking him for coming over, saying, "I just wanted to spend a little time going through these numbers with you again and see if we can come up with a plan of action."

"That sounds great to me," Frank replied. "I'm hoping we can make some sense out of this."

Jack left his desk and went to the whiteboard, drawing a diagram to point out the report's inconsistencies. This led to an in-depth discussion of how the significant amount of CPU memory the operating system was expending did not add up to the expenses the report allocated to all jobs. Frank and Jack discussed this for well over an hour, each adding more details to the whiteboard.

Finally, the discussion let up, and they stood back from their written conclusions on the board to summarize.

"It's almost as though jobs are running that are not accounted for at all," Frank opened up first.

"I completely agree with you," Jack replied. "But I think we need to bring someone else in to give us a third opinion. At least we can convince ourselves that we're not chasing some phantom reporting bug."

Frank thought about it for a second, then replied, "I think that's a great idea, but it has to be someone we trust and who can tread lightly on this. "

"I have just the guy for this," Jack offered. "John Jeffers — the military liaison to our office. I've worked with him extensively in the past and have a great deal of respect for him."

Frank quickly answered, "I've worked with him a little too. I think he's a good choice."

Jack finished this by saying, "All right, I'll see what his availability is along with yours, and I'll set something up as soon as possible and let you know. "

With that, they had their plan in place for the next step.

• • • •

After the meeting with Frank, Jack went straight to his calendar to see when he could set up a meeting with all of them. Everyone's week was jam-packed, with the only readily available time during lunch hour the following day. Jack thought it might be easier to approach Jeffers about his and Frank's conclusions over lunch, anyway. With that, he sent out an invitation for the three of them to talk things over.

The three met for lunch in the on-site cafeteria, where they could have a private discussion and no one would suspect a thing — after all, this was the CIA; confidential conversations were part of everyday business.

Jack wanted to get right down to it.

"Over the last couple of days, Frank and I have been discussing some irregularities with the quantum lab reporting. We'd like you to look at it as a third opinion to see what you think. I want to note that we think this is a delicate matter; I want to keep it quiet."

John thought things over for a minute before replying. "I would love to help out. I have been working on the quantum lab project from the technology side for a while, and I'm pretty familiar with its capabilities. I also understand the need to be discreet."

"Thanks," Jack smiled, "I appreciate it. I know you'll be a great help to us."

Frank added to the conversation, "I will get you all the data, John, and forward you my notes too; that should be plenty to get you started."

John nodded. "I'll get going as soon as you give me the data and get back to you once I've reviewed everything."

With that, they ended the discussion about the project and went into the usual small talk, eating their lunch and trying to keep the mood as light as possible.

Jack would wait to hear from Jeffers after he finished analyzing the data, and they would meet again to figure out what the next logical steps would be. Jack also felt a little uneasy, even though he completely trusted Jeffers; bringing more people into this and insinuating there might be something wrong in the quantum lab was certainly not a situation he wanted.

. . . .

That evening, Jack and Lucy were having dinner at home. Jack was spending more and more time thinking about the quantum lab's problems and whether he should press ahead with Frank and Jeffers. He wanted to bring the subject up to Lucy, putting it believably so that he might get her support.

He opened the conversation, hinting to Lucy that some issues at work were bothering him. He wanted to dive into the details and layout his case, but before he could, Lucy cut him off, giving him a kind look.

"Listen, I know some type of issue at work is really bothering you. I also know that you want to tell me about it to get my opinion, but just know that I'm supporting your cause. I just really don't want to know the details; I completely trust you to make the right decision. That's why I married you. I can always depend on you to think things through."

Jack was stunned by her words.

"Thanks, I didn't expect to hear that from you, and I guess you saved yourself a speech from me. I'm sorry if I've been a bit distracted lately; I am dealing with some things that are really bothering me. I know I have to press deeper into this, even if some risk is involved. "

Lucy laughed, "Good, I'm glad we had this talk. "

Feeling more at ease, they continued their dinner. Jack was pretty confident at this point that he needed to continue along the path with Frank and Jeffers, but he would once again file this away for the evening and confirm it during his morning run.

The run was short and focused the following morning. It didn't take Jack long to decide to press ahead with Frank and Jeffers; they would cautiously move forward and figure out what was behind the quantum lab's problems, no matter the consequences.

Jack didn't realize at this point what a dangerous decision he had just made.

ERIC FRICK

14

Chapter 3 Lucy's Discovery

Monday morning and Lucy was hard at work, getting things ready for the workweek at Senator Graben's office. She reviewed the senator's busy schedule and attempted to resolve conflicts for the week — something she always found quite challenging. She had almost finished when the senator buzzed her desk and asked her to come to his office, which is right down the hall from hers.

She hurried and opened the door, noticing he was talking to someone on the phone. Still, he waved to her to come in, and she could tell the conversation was winding up. She approached closer, hearing him say, "That sounds great. I look forward to seeing you on Friday. Good talking to you."

The senator hung up the phone, smiled, and said, "Happy Monday; I hope everything is going well and you had a great weekend."

"The weekend went by quickly as usual, but it was nice to relax from the hectic pace here, just for a little while," Lucy replied.

Graben laughed, "Well, I don't think the pace will slow down much this week, as the calendar seems jam-packed as it normally is. I called you in because I need you to fit one more meeting into my calendar. I was talking to Alex Brun on the phone just now; he's coming in on Friday morning at ten."

Lucy quickly shot back, "I just reviewed your calendar, and I know that time slot is open for Friday. I'll also make sure nothing else competes for that time."

"Lucy, what would I do without you?" Graben replied, ruffling through some papers on his desk.

Lucy smiled, "Thanks; it's always nice to start a Monday with a compliment! Those are sometimes hard to come by on Capitol Hill."

Graben told her he was meeting to discuss collaboration with high technology initiatives between industry and government, such as the quantum computing project.

This immediately raised Lucy's interest since Jack was the project manager. She wondered if he'd eventually be involved with whatever Brun and Graben would discuss and what the consequences would be for him. She chuckled to herself, thinking that it was just more meetings for Jack — something he despises.

With that thought, Lucy asked the senator, "Is there anything else you need from me this morning? I will email you the schedule revisions for the week, as well as some briefing notes for a couple of the high-level meetings."

"That's all I have for now," Graben replied. "I'll see you at the staff meeting in about an hour."

With that, Lucy thanked him and headed back to her own office to continue preparing for the weekly staff meeting.

. . . .

That Friday morning, Lucy sat at her desk, thinking about how quickly the workweek had gone. One of the things she liked about this job was that it was never dull, and the time passed quickly. She had worked at several jobs before this, where she'd had a lot of idle time and found it difficult to be motivated in those positions.

It was just before ten, and Lucy's phone rang to inform her that Alex Brun had arrived for his meeting with Senator Graben. She told the receptionist to send Mr. Brun to the senator's office and messaged Senator Graben to inform him that he was on his way.

Several minutes later, Graben asked Lucy to come back to his office. She immediately went down the hall and knocked on the door. When the senator told her to enter, she saw a very well-dressed man standing next to the senator behind his desk. He wore a very expensive suit, and she could tell he had carefully picked out all the accessories that went with it. After guiding so many visitors to the senator's office, Lucy had developed the ability to sum them up based on the type of clothing they wore. From what she saw, she could tell this was a man who paid a lot of attention to detail and liked to surround himself with quality things in his life.

Senator Graben spoke. "Lucy, I would like you to meet Alex Brun. Alex and I have been friends for a very long time."

Alex jumped in, saying, "It's very nice to meet you, Lucy; the senator has said so many nice things about you that I feel like I know you already."

"Wow, two compliments in one week," Lucy replied. "I think that's a record for me!"

They all laughed.

"Yes, that doesn't happen very often around here on Capitol Hill," Senator Graben commented. "If I were you, Lucy, I would go with the flow and accept the compliments."

Alex spoke up, "I'm excited to meet with the senator today to discuss some aspects of high technology projects he's working on. I'm exceptionally interested in the work your husband is doing with the quantum computing lab. It really does have enormous potential for the private high-tech industry in the United States."

Brun went on to say, "From what the senator has told me, your husband has done an outstanding job managing the lab. I hope to meet him someday to discuss it further."

His comments took Lucy aback since he seemed to know quite a bit about the computing lab and Jack. However, she was not overly surprised as it was such a high-profile project, and Jack was in a similarly high-profile position, spending quite a bit of time in the technical community.

Lucy smiled to herself and thought about what she might say to Jack about this meeting. Most of the time, Jack and Lucy had a policy not to bring home the details of their day jobs, focusing on building their relationship and lives together instead. Both with very complex and demanding jobs, there was no sense in bringing all that stress home every evening.

After exchanging a few more pleasantries, she said, "I realize you have a lot to talk about in a limited amount of time, so I'll take my leave. It was very nice to meet you, Mr. Brun."

"Thank you so much for setting all the details of this meeting up," Brun replied. "I look forward to my discussion with the senator. It was very nice to meet you."

· · · ·

Lucy left the senator's office and returned to her own to finish some outstanding items and wrap up the workweek. Even though her office was several doors down from the senator's, she could still sometimes overhear certain conversations, particularly if both their doors were open. She would not consciously try to overhear things but occasionally picked something up when people came and went from the senator's office.

Now, she could hear Alex Brun leaving the senator's office, giving his goodbyes. At the tail end of the conversation, she overheard Brun saying, "Victor, thank you so much for having me down today; I'm thrilled the fast track is going so well."

Lucy thought this was odd since she had never heard of this project. As she worked so closely with the senator, she knew about most of the projects he was involved with. She didn't put too much thought into it since many projects were classified, so she didn't have access to all of them. Still, she would store the unusual project's name in the back of her mind.

· · · ·

The following week, Lucy was busy helping Senator Graben prepare for a closed-door meeting with the Senate Intelligence Committee. These meetings usually required a lot of preparation and would dominate the week's activities. Lucy needed to put in a lot of overtime and work late into the evenings during these weeks, helping the senator prepare and juggle all the remaining priorities coming in and out of his office.

On Monday morning, while Lucy worked on some preparations, Graben messaged her and asked her to come into his office to help. She chuckled to herself that it was only Monday morning, and he was already asking for help with this month's meeting. It was going to be a long, hard week.

Once she arrived, Senator Graben said, "Thanks for popping down here so quickly. I have a few questions on some slides that I would like your input on."

"No problem," Lucy replied, "I was working on the slides only a few minutes ago, so they're still pretty fresh in my mind."

The senator had some general questions about the presentation's flow. Since Lucy had to spend some time working on this, she answered his questions and reassured him that all the information was correct. They were almost done when he questioned her on something further.

"I see this detailed list of expenditures on slide five. I want to make sure I have included everything here — especially anything from the black program side."

The black programs were accounted for separately since they were highly classified and not published as line-item expenditures in the budget's non-classified portion. Meetings with the Senate Intelligence Committee routinely dealt with these matters, meaning special attention to the details had to be made to ensure they were accurate.

"I'm not exactly sure what you're asking about on that slide," Lucy said, her brow furrowing slightly. She stepped behind his desk to get a closer look at the notes.

Graben seemed satisfied with the details she provided him and took the opportunity to jot down a few notes, adding a little more background during the presentation.

While behind his desk, a Post-it just happened to catch Lucy's eye, jumbled in with the rest of the preparation notes. It said in all capital letters, "ACCOUNT FOR FT." She immediately thought of Alex Brun's comments from the previous Friday about fast track; could that be FT?

Lucy was busy every day and late into the evening for the rest of that week, helping the senator with last-minute preparations for the Intelligence Committee meeting. It seemed like this would never end, but finally, they finished late on Wednesday evening, and Graben was ready for his Thursday morning meeting.

The senator packed up all the papers he needed and headed off for the midmorning session that morning. Lucy felt like a weight had been lifted off her shoulders and went to the break room to make herself a midmorning snack and a fresh cup of coffee.

She started to move on to a new set of tasks once she returned to her desk and began organizing her ideas of where to head next. Since it was almost the end of the week and most of it had been so busy with the meeting preparations, Lucy was ready for a new line of thinking.

. . . .

While thinking about everything she needed to finish by the end of the week, Lucy's mind returned to the fast track project. She quickly determined that she had a bit of time where she might be able to poke around and look at some of fast track's details.

Lucy began looking through some classified budget reports and noticed many expenditures and consulting invoices reported during the last quarter, billed from Mac Industries, the Nevada corporation.

Although these invoices were not tied to a specific project such as fast track, it seemed reasonable they might be related. Extensive knowledge was required to link accounted-for expenditures with specific highly classified projects. Lucy had a level of security clearance but not for many programs the senator was involved with.

Still, after working here for many years and helping with the budget process, she had developed the ability to make specific connections about various expenditures with particular projects.

In this case, it did not seem like anything was out of the ordinary. These expenditures appeared to fall in line with many other line items in this portion of the intelligence budget. Lucy had done enough digging to satisfy her curiosity, and it seemed like there was no smoking in here; it was part of the routine Intelligence Committee budget.

With that, she moved on to other pressing items at hand, though she would still remember the name "fast track" and the Nevada corporation's associated bills.

Jack began testing in the quantum lab to determine what was going on with the reporting system. He looked through the system scheduler and the scripts in place to produce the monthly reports. It has been a while since he had looked at these, and he wanted to verify that all the configurations were correct.

The CIA lab ran on Linux, and Jack was an expert at administering and modifying the operating system. He had worked with Linux for many years and held several certifications highlighting his expertise, as well as writing many articles and blog posts on highly technical subjects related to it.

He gathered information he could research later, so he started making a folder of different files and scripts to look at in more detail on his development system. Jack delved further into the archive system to look at changes made to the scheduler files over the last couple of months and gathered some system performance logs, reviewing usage trends in the central processing unit and system memory.

With all the details he had gathered, he could get a complete snapshot of what had gone on in the lab over the last few months. He could then compare these against the monthly reports for any discrepancies. Jack created a large zip file and copied it to his notebook computer to continue his research at home.

Once home, Jack performed a more in-depth analysis of the files. It did not take him long to find significant discrepancies between the detailed and reporting files. The management reporting system published these to management monthly, who used them to assess the lab's health and productivity.

It did not take Jack long to conclude that someone had compromised the reporting process and that the published report's information did not accurately reflect the lab's actual activity. It made him feel better, but he wasn't about to go on some type of witch hunt. Still, there was some real cause for concern with the discrepancies.

There was definitely something going on in the lab, and the amount of processing was almost exponentially steadily increasing.

• • • •

After a detailed review of the system logs, Jack was confident the reports had been altered or jobs were somehow being excluded. He packaged up what he had found to communicate it to Frank and Jeffers.

With that thought process over, Jack designed a new reporting mechanism — one very difficult to trace so that no one would find the changes. It also needed to be secure so that only he, Frank, and Jeffers could unlock the encryption. Because the software would encrypt the files, no one would know what they're looking at, even if they found it — not unless they had access to the keys.

Since the CIA lab ran Linux, it was possible to change the kernel to alter its behavior. These were tricky modifications to make since the kernel was the heart of the operating system, and any mistakes could severely impact the system. Jack, however, was an expert. With a small patch, he could write operational parameters to a protected area of memory and provide an interface to his new encrypted backend reporting system.

Since he now had the basic design in his head, Jack detailed the design and flushed out any potential problems. After that, he began writing some code and testing the patch on the development system he had access to. After a couple of days, Jack began seeing some success and sent a message to Frank, detailing what he had done.

Jack had forgotten how much he enjoyed programming and how fast time went by when working on a technical matter. He much preferred this type of work over the usual management board of personnel issues, budgets, and meetings.

The only major problem Jack faced at this point was figuring out how to deploy the software into the production environment with no one knowing about it yet. He decided he would work out that part of the plan later with Frank and Jeffers at their next meeting.

· · · ·

Since Jack and Lucy enjoyed their last dinner out so much, they went again without letting months pass. They returned to their favorite Italian place in Georgetown and tried to recreate the success they'd had.

However, once they sat down, neither of them was clearly in the same cheerful mood as the last time they'd had dinner out together. Jack had progressively been more distant and seemed engaged, with something else constantly on his mind. Lucy had noticed this over the last few days but had said nothing to her husband.

While thinking this over, Lucy opened the conversation.

"Jack, I realized I cut you off the other day when you wanted to talk about some problems you were dealing with at work. I'm sorry; I realize something is truly bothering you, and I'd like us to talk about it."

"I'm sorry if I've been so distant lately," Jack replied, "but yes, a lot is going on at work right now, and I'm just trying to sort it all out."

Lucy knew of the potentially sensitive information Jack was dealing with and carefully worded her reply. "I realize you're not at liberty to discuss a lot of things you work with, but if I can help...I just want to let you know I'm here for you."

Jack drew a deep breath. "Thanks, I appreciate that; it means more than you know. I have been dealing with some financial irregularities coming out of the backup lab, and I can't account for them. It's almost as though somebody has administrative access to the system and is running jobs and removing them from accounting."

"Have you talked to Jeff about this?"

Jack quickly scoffed, "Hell no, I don't trust Jeff at all. I actually have my suspicions about him; I think he may be involved."

Lucy laughed, "Okay, I get it; you don't have to go any further."

"Frank's helping me out with this as well, and he's finding some substantial expenditures associated with the backup lab."

Lucy seemed intrigued by the statement and followed up with, "I didn't know there even *was* a backup lab. When did you build this?"

· · · ·

Lucy's face turned white when Jack mentioned the lab's location. It seemed too much of a coincidence that she had found these strange expenditures and correspondence through Mac Industries in Nevada just last week.

She broke her rule of not talking shop with Jack and asked him, "Have you ever heard of a project called 'fast track'?"

Jack looked puzzled. "No, I haven't. Why do you ask?"

"Senator Graben's had several meetings related to the quantum lab and gathered some data to present to the Senate Intelligence Committee. I accidentally picked up some references to a project with that name. I did a bit of digging, even though I probably shouldn't have, and found that this project had a relationship to a company called Mac Industries. I tied it to several large invoices in Nevada."

Jack seemed to perk up when Lucy mentioned this information. She thought about telling him about Alex Brun, but she had perhaps already said more than she should have. She also felt a little guilty about using their private time to talk about work.

"Thanks for sharing that," Jack replied. "Also, thank you for letting me at least get a little of this off my chest. It has really helped just letting you know that there's nothing else bothering me besides this crazy thing at work."

Lucy laughed, "Once again, I'm sorry for shutting you down on this conversation a few days ago. If that ever happens again, press me a little harder."

With that, they both smiled at each other lovingly and noted that they had both violated their family rule of talking about work at dinner. After that, the conversation returned to their normal light conversation and away from serious work-related discussion.

Lucy vowed to continue her research about fast track and Mac Industries. There were far too many coincidences at this point for it not to lead to something.

· · · ·

The morning after dinner, Jack got up a little earlier since he still had a lot on his mind and needed the run to help sort things out. The weather cooperated, and it was a perfect morning for a run — a little chilly out, but just the kind of weather for pushing yourself really hard.

After Lucy had told him about Mac Industries, Jack had told himself that he would tell Frank about it and that this might be another piece in the quantum computing lab puzzle.

Still, it worried him that Lucy had now become involved. Jack laughed to himself, thinking he was letting his imagination run away with him. He almost scoffed at the idea that Lucy could be in potential danger. However, after a while, his thought process shifted to the dangerous types of people in the world and the constant threats the US government continually faced. In these days of terror, people really had no idea of the type of people they might be up against.

It did not take long for Jack's mind to clear on his run, and he quickly came up with a plan of action. He would contact Frank and Jeffers to let them know what he had found out and update them on the patch he was working on. By this time, he was more confident of their plan of action, but he still had some lingering doubt on how this could affect his career.

Chapter 5 Jack's Chance Encounter

Jack was having a routine day; he'd had a perfect run in the morning, his head was feeling clear, and he was incredibly energetic.

At work, his schedule was unusually very light, and he wanted to use the opportunity to get some things done in his personal life that he had been letting slide.

The first order of business was to clear any remaining items from his calendar to ensure nothing lingered for the rest of that day. It took him about twenty minutes to go through that morning's messages, respond to a few staff inquiries, and reach a point where everything seemed wrapped up.

Jack headed into the break room to get his mid-morning coffee before finishing up the rest of that day's items and saw Frank, who was pouring his own cup.

"Funny I should find you here," Frank began, "I was thinking about taking a long lunch today."

That was code for Frank wanting to sneak out to the golf course and his way of inviting Jack.

"Well, great minds think alike," Jack replied, "but unfortunately, I cleared my afternoon to take care of some personal errands, and I really can't put them off any longer."

"Sorry to hear that — the weather is absolutely perfect today to squeeze in a quick round," said Frank as he made a swinging motion, pretending to hold a golf club.

Jack chuckled, "Consider this a rain check. I promise we will go out again soon."

Frank sipped his coffee. "I'll hold you to it! What errands are you running, anyway?"

"I need to go shopping for Lucy's birthday, and I've been putting it off," Jack replied.

"Got it. Make sure you get Lucy something nice; she deserves it for putting up with you!" Frank chuckled.

"You bet," Jack smiled back as he left the kitchen and headed back to his office.

Jack took his time sipping his coffee and ambled past Yanko's office. He noticed someone entering from a distance, the door quickly shutting. Jack didn't think it was anything unusual, but he had never seen the person before, which was surprising — when working inside the CIA headquarters, visitors were somewhat of a rare occasion.

Quickly making his way back to his office, Jack drank the rest of his coffee and finished that day's work activities so he could go shopping in the afternoon. He completed his tasks a little quicker than he expected and grabbed an early lunch, shooting a quick email to Yanko to remind him he would be out this afternoon and that he could message him if anything came up.

. . . .

His workday behind him, Jack was set to go about his business with his early lunch and shopping trip when he realized that the driver in front was none other than the stranger who'd gone into Yanko's office.

After a couple of turns, Jack was still behind the stranger's car as they moved closer to the city. Curious about who he might be, he followed a little further to determine where the man was going. There was certainly no harm in going for an afternoon drive, Jack rationalized.

The stranger pulled into a rental car return near Union Station in the city's heart. Jack immediately knew then that he was out of town and had just come in for the day to visit Yanko. On a complete whim, Jack parked near Union Station and went into the terminal to see if he could spot him and figure out what train he was taking.

. . . .

Once inside, Jack began second-guessing his decision — after all, he was not a field operative but a computer scientist with an academic background; following someone and stalking them was way outside his comfort zone. He even chuckled when he thought about it. Still, since Jack was already in the terminal, he decided to get something to eat, spotting a potbelly sandwich shop and grabbing a seat.

He was just getting settled when the stranger he had been following walked by. Jack had an unobstructed view of him and could easily see which direction he was heading. Without ordering anything, Jack got up and followed him, his rational line of thinking evaporating entirely.

Careful not to get too close, it became apparent that the stranger was heading to the train going to New York City. Jack thought of an excuse to take the trip. He already had the afternoon off to go shopping — why not do it in New York? He could visit his friend Jay there and pick up something nice for Lucy's birthday at his jewelry shop. He had not seen Jay in a long time and thought this could be a fun day trip.

Even though Jack knew deep down that he was kidding himself, he used his newfound excuse to buy a train ticket from one of the easy-to-use kiosks. At least for the time being, he did not focus on the crazy aspect of his unexpected day trip but on seeing his friend again. Jay was one of his lifelong college buddies from Ohio, and they had spent many fun times golfing and drinking together. Even if the driving force behind the last-minute trip was off the wall, Jack reasoned that it would be good to meet up and connect with him again.

The trip was about three-and-a-half hours, arriving in New York around 3.30pm. Jack figured that he could read on the train or catch up on some quantum computing research. Since the Amtrak train had Wi-Fi and Jack had his notebook computer with him, he was all set for the trip. He could also use the time to shop online for some ideas for Lucy's birthday present, which was the real purpose of this trip.

Jack quickly stopped by the press stand for a newspaper and a sandwich for lunch before hopping on the train, thinking he could spend the time reading the paper if he became tired of surfing the internet.

· · · ·

Jack started looking for a seat once he boarded the train. He looked up and happened to see the stranger sitting in the front car. It just so happened that a seat was at the back of the same car, and Jack quickly took it and settled in for the ride to New York. It had been a while since he had been on the train, and he was pleasantly surprised by the comfortable seat and was actually looking forward to the trip.

Soon, the train pulled out of the station. Jack glanced toward the front of the car and noticed the stranger had opened up his computer, seemingly hard at work. Jack was not watching the stranger's every move; he just happened to glance up and see what he was doing.

Just as Jack had opened up his newspaper and began reading, the conductor stopped to check his ticket. He seemed very friendly when asked Jack if he was heading back home.

"No," Jack smiled, "just heading up to New York for a little sightseeing and shopping today."

"Well, you picked a great day for it," the conductor replied. "The weather is fantastic in New York today."

"Yes, not many days are nicer than today. I'm really looking forward to the trip and spending some time in the city. "

The conductor quickly checked his ticket stub and then replied, "Thanks so much, and I hope you have a great day in the city!" and went on his way to check the next set of tickets and passengers.

After the conductor had left, Jack realized he was pretty hungry and remembered he had bought a sandwich and a bottle of water at the station in Washington. He reached into his bag, remembering that he had thrown in an apple earlier in the week that he never ate. The pre-made sandwich surprised Jack; it was actually pretty good as he realized he could take his time since he would have a long train ride up to New York.

After finishing up his lunch, he opened the newspaper and caught up on some of the day's events. Soon, Jack felt sleepy and dozed off, the combination of the nice big sandwich he just ate and the moving train a perfect environment for falling asleep.

Jack's sleep was short but heavy, and when he woke, he was confused for a brief second about where he was. After a few seconds, he quickly regained his composure and started to seriously second-guess what he was doing.

Still, he justified the trip so that he could go shopping in one of his favorite cities and would have some time to do a little strolling around on such a great day. However, in the back of his mind, he still felt guilty about how he had incrementally talked himself into taking this trip without really thinking it through.

After about twenty minutes, the train pulled into the station in New York City, and the passengers exited onto the platform. Luckily, Jack could flow with the crowd and stay a comfortable distance behind the stranger. It was relatively easy to tail him at a distance. Thankfully, he only had to walk a short way to see that the stranger was heading to the limousine area.

Luckily for Jack, he could easily pick up a cab from a queue of waiting passengers here. He looked over and saw that the stranger had stopped to pick up a newspaper and had headed toward a seemingly pre-arranged limousine since the driver greeted the stranger with a handshake, and they seemed to know each other.

. . . .

Jack quickly hailed a cab while the stranger was getting into his limousine, thinking how lucky it was for it to be right next to the limousine line.

Once in the cab, he asked the driver to follow the limousine. The cabbie didn't hesitate, asking Jack for an extra $50 to do it.

Jack grumbled to himself about the extra money, but it was expected, and he was happy that the cab driver didn't want a long discussion about it. Jack thought that this was probably not all that unusual given cab drivers' years of driving customers around — especially in places like New York City. And it was clear from the moment they set off that the cabbie had done this before.

The limousine stopped in front of a vast, luxurious-looking house after about a fifteen-minute drive. Jack told the cabbie to pull over about a half a block away, just up the street. He quickly settled the bill with the cab driver, thanking him for helping him out. The driver took the money in silence; a cabbie was also smart enough not to ask questions.

Jack looked down the street and noticed the stranger had gone into the house. Once the limousine pulled away, he walked down the street and walked past the front of the house, noting the address he would put in his cell phone to look up later. He thought about taking a picture of the house but felt that it would draw too much attention. This would be a good move on his part.

. . . .

Once Jack had the address, he went to his favorite jewelry store close to the stranger's house — Margo Manhattan Jewelry, which his good friend Jay Hafner owned.

Jay had been in the high-stress commercial world for years and was quite successful. One day, he became fed up with working for other people and decided to set up his own store. Jay had collected and sold jewelry on the side for a while, and with his deep background in sales, his style fit well with New York City.

It turned out to be a short walk to the store. Jack entered and immediately saw his friend, who called out to him, "I just never know who is going to walk in the door. How the hell are you, Jack?!"

"Jay, it's great to see you again!" he replied. "I can't believe the difference leaving the corporate rat race has made on you. You look great!"

Jay sighed, "You know you can look a lot better when you can sleep at night, all night!"

"I'll take your word for it!" Jack nodded.

They took the opportunity over the next half hour to catch up on the last couple of years and kicked around some old war stories from college. To both of them, those stories never got old, but they seemed to grow as the stories were stretched over the years.

Finally, his friend said, "I'm sure you're not here just to tell old stories."

" I wish I could say I was," Jack began. "I'm in New York on business for the day and thought I'd stop by to see if I could pick something for my wife for her birthday tomorrow. I knew you were the best and could help me out."

Jay went immediately into sales mode, asking, "What exactly are you looking for?"

Jack said he was looking for a bracelet, and the two reviewed several suggestions. Jay quickly narrowed down the selection based on Jack's parameters and price, glad he could do business with his friend. Jack hated going to jewelry stores; he always felt he was getting ripped off. He made the final selection, and Jay quickly took care of the purchase.

Relieved to do the only thing he really needed to that day, Jack warmly gave his thanks. "You are a lifesaver, Jay!"

"No worries," Jay replied. "I hope we can get together more often and keep in touch."

They both chatted for a few more minutes. Jack handed him a card and told him to give him a call the next time he was in DC.

· · · ·

After saying goodbye, Jack jumped into a cab and headed back to the station to take the train back to DC. After a quick ride, Jack arrived at the terminal, noting that people were already boarding for the trip home. He was happy to get this trip over as soon as possible because he felt guilty about the entire process.

Jack quickly made his way to the train and boarded, pleased to see it wasn't nearly as crowded as the one he had taken earlier in the day. Because of this, he could find a great seat and quickly settled in.

Now that he had gone to all this effort, with the house number and street clearly typed out in his phone, Jack wanted to know who this person was. He got out his laptop, hoping he could quickly figure it out with just the address. He knew he could find the owner's address by going to city records and checking the property title, but tired from the day's journey, he quickly typed it into Google, knowing it was probably a long shot. He was surprised to see the address had a lot of hits and identified the property owner as Alex Brun.

Brun was a well-known Washington lobbyist and insider. Jack thought it only a little strange that someone like him had visited the CIA, but not highly unusual since he represented so many high-profile industrial companies, including some defense contractors.

Jack started to feel silly after finding this out. He had gone to all this effort, only to tail an innocent person he had seen leaving his boss's office. He realized that this entire trip was completely out of character for him. He had worked hard to get his dream job, and now he was doing inane things like this that might actually endanger his career. He also now doubted any link between Brun and the irregularities going on in the backup lab.

Feeling that he was perhaps taking this too far, Jack thought it best to leave things alone for a while. He also felt guilty about not telling Lucy the truth about this trip.

One of Jack's unique qualities was the ability to turn things off in his mind and not think about them for a while. It had taken him years to develop the skill, but it had served him well in many situations that would've previously pushed him into a full-blown panic. It was like a switch he could turn on in his head. He did this now as he made his way to the dining car to get something to eat and enjoy the rest of his trip.

THE RISE OF THE DEEP STATE

35

After Jack's visit to New York, Alex Brun was in his home office, going through the previous day's video surveillance. He and the rest of the Deep State organization were paranoid about their privacy and security, so they'd naturally had a sophisticated surveillance system installed in Alex's brownstone mansion. He routinely reviewed the footage for anything suspicious. Facial recognition software was also recently installed in the system, highlighting any unusual traffic in front of the brownstone. Alex was immediately interested in one particular event that had occurred the previous day — the surveillance system noted that it was Jack Brown, the well-known computer scientist.

After a quick Google search, Alex discovered that Jack was the head of the quantum computer lab at CIA headquarters in Langley, Virginia. Alex thought the location was just a coincidence at first but decided that he needed to investigate further. He planned to visit CIA headquarters later in the week, hoping to meet up with this Jack Brown to see what he was up to.

Alex immediately called Yanko to set up a quick routine meeting, careful not to tip him off about who he had seen.

• • • •

Alex took the 6am train from New York City to Washington DC. He always preferred train travel for this trip over flying; it was a much more relaxing trip, and it allowed him some time to think about his projects. He could also get a little extra sleep on the journey to freshen up for the day. He had taken this trip so many times that he had the routine down pat. He would catch the limo from his home that would take him to Penn Station and then take the early train to DC, which would get him in around 9:30. This schedule would leave him plenty of time to get to Langley for a lunchtime meeting.

In most cases, Alex would hang around for the rest of the day, then take the late train home or book a hotel room and return the next morning. In this case, he had an 11:30 meeting scheduled with Yanko. He calculated it would only take fifteen or twenty minutes, so he could take the opportunity to swing by and meet Jack Brown and see where the conversation goes.

• • • •

The trip was uneventful, and Alex Brun arrived like clockwork just minutes before his scheduled meeting with Yanko, who came to the lobby to sign him in and escort him to his office — standard policy for CIA meetings.

"How was your trip down here?" Yanko asked.

"I've done this so many times I could do it in my sleep," Brun chortled. "In fact," he added, "many times, I *have* done it in my sleep!"

They made their way up to Yanko's office to start their meeting. Alex opened the conversation by saying, "I didn't come down for a particular reason; I just wanted to check to make sure everything was on schedule and that you weren't having any issues."

Yanko seemed extremely relaxed this morning as he replied, "Everything is on track, and the job queue is steadily increasing in the backup lab. All the jobs successfully completed with no errors, and we seem to be in good shape. We plan to steadily increase production over the next few weeks."

Alex made a happy tapping sound on Yanko's desk. "Fantastic," he replied with a grin. "I'm delighted to hear this. Being on schedule with production is extremely important at this stage, particularly with the primaries just starting in a few weeks. Mac will be very pleased to hear it."

Yanko jumped in, "I'm glad you're both happy with the current progress."

Though Alex had made excuses to set up this meeting with Yanko, he was still relieved to hear the progress report. He had listened to all he had wanted to hear, interested in cutting the meeting short to see if he could meet Jack Brown.

"Mr. Yanko," Alex began, "I don't want to take any more of your time. I'm delighted we met, and I just really wanted to connect to make sure everything was still on point. Hey," he added, pretending it was an afterthought, "the last time I was here, you were going to introduce me to your lab manager, Jack Brown. Since I have a little extra time, maybe I could meet him now?"

Unsuspecting, Yanko was happy to comply. "Of course; his office is right down the hall — I'll take you there and see if he's in."

• • • •

Jack finished up some routine email correspondence and stood from his chair to head down the hall and grab a cup of coffee when he heard a knock on the door. He looked up and saw Yanko and, to his immediate surprise, the stranger, Alex Brun, standing in his doorway. It horrified him at the prospect that Brun was here, and he instantly thought about his ad hoc trip to New York the previous week. Before Jack could say anything, Yanko began by saying, "Jack, I would like to introduce you to Alex Brun. Alex is a good friend of mine from college and just stopped by to see how I was doing. He mentioned he had seen an article of yours online and was interested in meeting you."

"Sorry to pop in unannounced, but I read your article last week," Brun quickly responded. "I thought that since I was here to talk to Jeff, I would take the opportunity to meet you. I don't know much about quantum computing, but I would love to learn about it from one of our nation's experts," he grinned and offered out a hand for Jack to shake. He did so willingly and, after taking a few moments to regain his composure, replied, "It's very nice to meet you. I'm always happy to talk about quantum computing any chance I get. Most people are sorry they asked about quantum computing because I just can't stop talking about it!"

Brun laughed and replied, "Well, since I'm a newbie in the field and don't know much about it, maybe you can dumb down the conversation so I can understand some of the concepts?"

"I would love to do that; it might be dumber than you think."

Brun began to pressure Jack further, possibly due to Yanko being present. Brun replied, "I know I'm an unscheduled visitor, but I'd be happy to take you to lunch someplace close by so that we can continue our conversation."

Although fearful of Brun's intentions, Jack knew this was the perfect opportunity to get to know a little more about him and perhaps further confirm he wasn't involved in the lab's reporting discrepancies. Jack replied, "It just so happens my schedule is very open this morning, so I'd be happy to grab lunch with you."

. . . .

Jack got his coat and locked his computer, and they headed off to Brun's rental car. "Where would you like to go?" Brun asked.

Jack thought about it for a moment. "There aren't a ton of options; anything close is in McLean." He then asked, "What type of food do you like?"

"I'm not really a picky eater," Brun answered after a brief pause, "but I wouldn't mind Italian if there's anything like that."

"I do know one place called Capri Ristorante Italiano. It's in McLean; it's really only a short drive from here, and they can probably get us in and out pretty quick."

They got into Brun's rental and headed to the restaurant. The weather had turned much better than the previous week, so they took the time to discuss it, both hoping that the winter weather would be mild this year. Jack was used to much worse weather in the winter, coming from Ohio, so it didn't really bother him. Brun told Jack that he really hated cold weather and looked for any opportunity to escape it.

"I could certainly use a trip to Florida too, at least to see the sun again," Jack laughed.

Fortunately, there was no wait at the restaurant, and they were seated right away. A position like Jack's didn't allow the opportunity to go out to lunch very often. Even though this was a slightly stressful situation for him, Jack still enjoyed the chance to get out and have an enjoyable meal for lunch.

The server promptly came over and took their drink order, returning several minutes later to ask if they had any questions about the menu. Jack ordered first — lasagna, a dish he'd ordered before several times, though he was by no means a regular here.

"Of course," the server replied before turning to Brun to ask if he was ready to order. He chose the linguine with clams and an appetizer of stuffed mushrooms, thanking the server and getting straight down to business with Jack.

As they talked, Jack could tell that Brun was obviously a well-connected, well-schooled Washington insider; he would have the entire lunch ritual with government offices down to a science. He also seemed eager to see what Jack knew about the quantum computing project.

Jack paused for a moment to collect his thoughts, then began. "Quantum computing is fundamentally new. It significantly differs from traditional computers using a binary computing model, which means specific complex problems that traditional computers have great difficulty with can be solved."

He waited a moment to see if Brun would interrupt before pressing on. "These problems could be complex simulations and difficult search algorithms. Quantum computing really does represent an exponential step forward in computing technology."

Brun finally nodded and stated. "I also understand that this technology has been difficult to perfect."

"Yes, exactly," Jack replied. "We can overcome most of those issues with our lab hardware's latest revisions. We are ready for prime time now!"

Brun seemed amazed, commenting, "That's exciting news. I don't want you to spend your entire lunch talking shop, though. Do you know where I can get more information? Is there someone I could meet near my home in New York City?"

Jack thought about it for a minute before replying, "Yes, actually — NYU has some excellent resources I could link you up with. I will make an introduction for you."

Appearing to be quite happy about this, Brun gushed his thanks. "We're lucky to have such great education resources in New York City! Have you ever been to Manhattan?"

Jack almost froze in his tracks — had Brun somehow spotted him in New York? Luckily, Jack already had a cover story. "Why, yes. As a matter of fact, I was up there just last week on a shopping trip."

"That's quite a way to travel for some shopping!" Brun laughed.

Jack quickly answered, "A friend of mine owns a jewelry shop in Manhattan, and I stopped by to get my wife an anniversary present."

Brun didn't seem entirely convinced as he asked, "Wow, that's great! What shop is it?"

Thankful he had taken the bait, Jack replied, "Margo Manhattan Jewelry."

This seemed to hit a chord with Brun. "Oh, really — that shop is very close to my home; I know it well."

Jack laughed and replied, "Wow, it's a small world! So close to where you live. It is a fantastic area."

Brun seemed satisfied with the story and no longer interested in pressing him for more information.

Noting the time, Jack suggested they head back to the office, where he had a meeting. Brun agreed and called for the server to bring the check. He insisted on paying, even though government employees are required to pay their way. Jack relented, as accepting a small lunch from a visitor was the least of his problems.

They jumped in Brun's rental car for the quick drive back to CIA headquarters. They had some light conversation about the Italian food and seemed to be clear on each other's intentions, as far as Jack was concerned. They pulled up to the entrance, where Brun extended a hand as Jack was about to get out. "It was really great to meet and have lunch with you. Perhaps we can do this again sometime?"

Jack returned the gratitude and made his way back to his office, feeling pretty good about the meeting now that the fear of Brun showing up at his office had disappeared.

Jack shouted, "Have a good trip back!" as Brun pulled away.

• • • •

As Alex Brun pulled away from CIA's headquarters, he determined he had plenty of time to make the afternoon train home and didn't need to spend the night in DC. He drove onto the George Washington Memorial Parkway heading out of Langley and immediately called James Mac.

James Mac was a well-known industrialist, hugely successful over the last several years, and had established a vast fortune. He started his career running a small industrial firm in Dayton, Ohio, specializing in hi-precision manufacturing. He eventually became an expert in process engineering and could inherently see flaws in any process, immediately improving them and using that ability to exponentially grow his business.

The overwhelming success got to him at some point. Playing by the rules and growing a mere twenty or thirty percent a year was no longer enough for Mac. Several years ago, he crossed the line and looked for ventures to grow his business on a global scale. During this, he became involved with Alex and Trucker, and they had formed a seed for the current plot in which they were involved.

The plot to form the Deep State project did not come as an overnight idea from Mack. It just naturally evolved as one project morphed into another. To grow his business globally on a level he knew, Mac would need to massively tilt the game in his favor. Alex stumbling onto the quantum computer lab and their entry into the project with Yanko seemed like a golden opportunity for this exact thing. The promise of unlimited power had incrementally seduced Mac along the way as this plot moved further and further toward reality.

Mac wasn't necessarily an evil man, and he certainly didn't start out that way. But as time passed and projects started succeeding, he gradually changed how he conducted business. Mac accepted practices that he would never have considered earlier in his career. It also probably didn't help that he had gone through a profoundly personal crisis with his wife, losing her to a hard-fought disease. It had hardened him along his life's journey until eventually, he had become relatively isolated from a social standpoint, just concentrating on his business. That isolation merely fed his need for growth and the drive to accumulate power.

The phone rang a few times, and Alex wondered if it would roll to voicemail when a voice suddenly hopped on.

"Alex, do you have something for me?"

"I made a quick trip to Langley to check out Jack Brown, the quantum computing lab's technical director," Alex replied. "I saw him on our facial recognition software in front of my brownstone last week. I had lunch with him to check out his situation and see if anything suspicious was going on." Alex paused briefly to make sure Mac was taking all this in. "There is nothing to worry about here; he is a typical computer nerd and doesn't know what's going on. I also met with Yanko; he said everything is on track and going in the right direction."

Alex could hear Mac chuckling on the other end of the line before he replied. "It looks like this thing is really moving in the right direction, and we're ready to gear up for big-time production —it sounds like everything's in order. Thanks for the update and for checking out Brown. Set up a meeting with Trucker and us at my place in Florida." With that, Mac ended the conversation, and Alex began his trip back to New York.

• • • •

With a successful morning meeting, Alex thought about the next phase of the project. He would have plenty of time to make the train, so he decided to have dinner somewhere in DC. He then made plans to find a private place for a call with Trent Hardway; he needed to make sure the money would be available for the project's next phase.

Trent was the project's money-laundering expert, whose nickname was 'the Trucker' for his uncanny ability to move enormous sums of untraceable money. Alex had used Trucker for years on these types of projects, but never anything on a massive scale like this. Now that the project was really heating up, Alex would need to have some detailed conversations with him, as well as setting up the meeting Mac had requested. They wanted to ensure Trucker set deep cover correctly so no one could trace what was really going on.

Before boarding his train, Alex set aside some extra time to call Trucker from the station lounge. Union Station had a pretty nice one, and Alex used it frequently. He got himself a cup of coffee, then made the call.

A loud voice answered after a couple of rings, "Trent Hardway here." One of the things Alex liked about dealing with Trucker is that he was extraordinarily businesslike and very efficient at what he did.

"This is Brun calling," Alex replied. "I'm just on my way back from a trip to DC and was calling to check in with you to see how things were going."

"I've got things moving," Trucker confirmed, "and everything is in place for the bigger operation. I put some encrypted files in the usual place for you to review; you can see for yourself the progress I've been making."

Everything about this day was falling into place for Alex, and it relieved him to hear the progress Trucker was making.

"The boss wants to meet at his usual spot down in Florida to go over all the last details before we really ramp up," Alex added.

"Sounds good; tell him to break out the good stuff when I get there. When would you like to meet?"

"As early as possible next week. Can you make Tuesday?"

"Of course," Trucker replied.

"Great, then we'll make this a one-day trip. I'll send the plane for you. See you in Florida next Tuesday." With that, Alex hung up and started making his way to the train for the trip back to Manhattan.

With the lab production increasing and the success of the scheduled jobs in the quantum computing lab, Alex was pleased that the project was moving along perfectly. The Deep State was now about to become a reality.

45

Chapter 7 The Information Leak

Jack was happy today was over. What had started as a routine day had suddenly transformed into a horrifying event when Brun had unexpectedly shown up in his office. Even though this had plenty of potential for problems, Jack felt relieved about the conversation, pretty confident Brun suspected nothing from him after their lunch.

Though Brun was no longer on his trail, Jack had some lingering doubts and knew it was necessary to get moving on doing something about the obvious crisis about to unfold. He wasn't sure exactly what to do, but he knew he needed help — he knew just the person for it.

As soon as he got to the office, Jack called Frank and Jeffers and asked them to check their morning schedules. They all had an opening later that morning, so Jack reserved a conference room for an eleven o'clock meeting with the two of them. One of the useful things about working for the CIA was that every conference room in the facility was secure, so he didn't need to worry about anybody eavesdropping on them.

• • • •

Frank, Jeffers, and Jack all promptly arrived at eleven. They dispensed with the usual small talk and got down to business right away.

Jack first told Frank and Jeffers about his trip to New York and how he discovered Alex Brun. He then told them about Brun's visit to the CIA and that they had gone to lunch, breaking down the detailed conversation and how they had left things. Jack wanted to know what they thought of the situation.

Frank was the first one to break the ice. "I know you felt like you put him off your trail and that he doesn't suspect you know anything about these rogue jobs running on the lab, but I worry he might be just putting on an act."

Jeffers quickly chimed in, "Yeah, Jack, I've seen these types my entire life, and I don't trust him at all. I think we need to get the ball clearly out of our court."

Jack thought about it for a moment before replying, "I agree with both of you. I have a really uneasy feeling about what's going on; it feels like I'm flying blind. We have no idea what those jobs are doing in the backup, but we do know that activity is regularly picking up."

As the accountant in the group, Frank routinely thought about setting up reporting for any type of project, and this was no exception. He was busy doodling something on his notepad when he looked up to comment.

"We really need a secure locking mechanism so we can detail what's happening with these jobs. We need to fix it so only we can access the logs through a series of passkeys and encryption. That way, we can at least have a look at what these jobs are doing and the resources they're consuming."

That idea sparked something in Jack, and he quickly interjected. "I've been working on something already! We can't really control their jobs, but if we can at least see what they're doing, we'll have visibility at what havoc these jobs might be causing. If you can design an encrypted logging backend, I'm pretty sure I can design a trojan horse to install in the lab to make it look like a routine operating system patch."

The group was making quick progress, Jeffers asking, "Can we cover our tracks when putting this type of software into the system?"

Frank replied, "Since I have administrative access, I should be able to cover all this as routine patching, maintenance, and backup activity. The problem is we will need physical access to the facility to install the software on-site."

"Can we access the lab with no one knowing we were there?" Jeffers asked Frank.

Jack replied, "We can, and I can cover our tracks since I have administrative access to the facility *and* all the lab's security controls itself. I can make it look like we were never there. The problem is with Nevada's air force base — I don't have access to any of that security. We will have to bypass it to get onto the base without being detected."

Jeffers thought about it for a moment before saying, "Leave that to me. I'm pretty sure I can get us onto the base undetected and get you to the facility building. The rest will be up to you."

"Okay, great," Frank said before adding, "The last thing we will need is a cover story to get the two of you close to the base and not raise any suspicion. Let me look at some events going on nearby and see if we can come up with something credible to get the two of you out there quickly."

They all agreed on the basic plan, which had fallen together very quickly. First, Frank would design an encryption algorithm for the system log files, then the script would copy them to a place they could access to monitor the backup quantum lab's activity. Next, Jack would design and install a patch as a routine maintenance job to cover the backup logs and encryption without raising suspicion at a system level. He would also arrange a cover story for he and Jeffers to travel somewhere in Nevada. Finally, Jeffers would devise a plan to get them onto the air force base undetected.

With each of them with their tasks to complete, they planned to meet several days later.

They all felt pretty good about the plan and thought they could pull all the elements together to get it moving quickly. But they hadn't addressed one area — the contact Jack had had with Brun several days earlier.

"I've been thinking a lot about this since our lunch meeting," said Jack after the other two brought up their concerns. "It's even bothered me to the point where I'm having trouble sleeping at night."

Ever since Jack and Lucy had compared notes about this, he'd had the idea to plant a leak in the community, implicating Senator Graben. Based on his conversations with Lucy, Graben was up to his neck in this plot; now might be the perfect opportunity to plant that seed so that Brun and his colleagues wouldn't ever consider Jack's involvement.

Jack shared this plan with the others. "Graben is clearly involved in this," he said. "I think it would really throw them off the trail if they doubt his loyalty."

Jeffers was quick to jump in, "I think that's a fantastic idea, and the sooner we can get it done, the better I'll feel."

"I love it, Jack," Frank nodded. "Do you know someone who can help us out?"

"I know someone in operations who could do this job in their sleep," Jack replied. "I also have plenty of material from Lucy that I can cut loose to the Times. It will look like the leak came directly from him."

That was the last item of detail filling in the plan's missing piece. The team felt pretty good about it all and, believing they had accounted for everything, they were ready to go.

• • • •

Jack immediately went to work on the first part of the plan to implement the information leak. He pulled together some relevant material about the quantum lab that was relatively harmless but clearly linked to Graben's office. Jack then contacted his friend in operations, who agreed to take care of the leak.

One of the great things about working with the CIA was that leaking information to the press was a routine operation, and they had tons of resources to make it happen quickly and effectively. Jack put his information together and gave it to his contact, who told him it would only take a day or so to get it to the Times.

Two days later, like clockwork, an article appeared on the front page. It gave some lousy press to Senator Graben's office and the quantum computer project, mentioning the waste of taxpayer money on a relatively immature technology. As far as government scandals went, this was certainly not a terrible incident. Still, it was a pretty deep embarrassment for both Graben and his office.

That same morning, Jack saw Yanko in the hallway as he headed back from getting his morning coffee. Yanko immediately stopped to ask Jack, "Hey, did you see Graben's giant gaff in the Times this morning?"

"I did," he replied, "it was pretty ugly for him. I can't believe he was stupid enough to tip off the Times."

Looking as though he'd already had way too much coffee, Yanko replied, "Well, he really stuck it to himself; our side of it seems pretty clean, and we don't have much of a problem. I've already talked to the director; he's very supportive."

"That's good news. I'm glad to hear it," Jack replied, attempting to head back to his desk and away from Yanko's questioning.

"What does Lucy have to say about all of this?" asked Yanko, stopping Jack dead.

He knew where this line of questioning was leading to and wondered how he could quickly cut off any suspicion on his wife and shut down Yanko cold. He actually thought about this somewhat on the drive into work this morning. Jack's reply was not much of a stretch of the truth at all.

"Lucy's had just about enough of Washington politics and Senator Graben in particular. I wouldn't be surprised if she made a move soon; she hasn't told me directly, but I know she's missing her family back in Ohio, and the work in the Senate is not exactly what she thought it would be."

Jack assumed Yanko would be pleased about this, knowing that if Lucy moved back to Ohio, Jack would quickly follow, and he would be rid of them for good. There was certainly a mutual dislike between the two men.

Still, Yanko knew to carefully offer a politically correct answer and replied, "I'm really sorry to hear that, Jack. I know this was Lucy's dream job, and she was really excited about working and the senator's office. I certainly understand wanting to be close to family, and there is no replacement for that. I hope things work out for both of you."

Jack was somewhat surprised by his boss's sincerity, but his evident despise for Jack would still be in the back of his mind. Jack also thought it prudent to plant the seed with Yanko that he might be leaving DC, and for a valid reason. It was yet another measure that would cover his trip to Nevada with Jeffers.

• • • •

The next day, Jack, Frank, and Jeffers met again to firm up the plan's details and to ensure they had not forgotten anything. Jack had been hard at work, putting his part of the plan together, and was anxious to update them.

The first thing they discussed was the cover story Jack had planned. He and Jeffers would fly to Nevada to attend an artificial intelligence conference in Las Vegas. Jack would present one of the sessions on some unclassified work he had been working on during the last year. Jack would also put a bit of a military spin on his presentation, so it was logical for Jeffers to attend too. They all agreed that this cover story seemed very reasonable and that nobody should doubt their trip.

Jack then briefed the group on the patch architecture he had designed to log system activity and provided a method that Frank's encryption program could interface to. He described the installation procedure he needed, stating that it would take just a few minutes. He also explained how he would modify all the system logs to ensure his visit would remain a secret.

Next, Frank laid out the details of the logging and encryption mechanism he had designed and how he would export the results to an area only they could access. The design would ensure they were getting accurate job information that nobody had altered in any way.

Finally, Jeffers briefed the group on his plan to get them on the air force base without detection. He had arranged a helicopter charter to fly them from Las Vegas to the base, and they would insert themselves from there, using the excuse that they were flying to Lake Mead for a nighttime tour and dinner — a typical daily charter. From there, they would fly from Lake Mead under the radar and get Jack into the lab undetected. Jack was a little uneasy about this part, but Jeffers assured him that the charter pilot he would hire was the best in the business.

Chapter 8 Mac, Alex, and Trucker Meet

Alex and Trucker arrived at Destin Executive Airport in Florida in the afternoon. They had flown in from New York on Mac's Gulfstream G550 personal jet. Though Alex had been on this airplane before, the luxury plane never got old.

A limousine greeted them as soon as they walked off the plane, taking them to Mac's beachfront home — a mere five-minute drive from the airport.

Someone immediately came out to help them with their luggage when they arrived. They had also brought their golf clubs since Mac had scheduled a round for the next day.

Once inside, the butler handling their baggage told them to make their way out to the back porch, where Mac was waiting.

The living room they entered had a large glass wall that could open entirely onto the back porch. The view was nothing short of spectacular, and the porch itself incorporated a complete outdoor kitchen with a pool and hot tub. It was an incredible setup.

Mac was sitting having a drink and smiled when he saw them both.

"I hope you had a smooth trip down here and didn't have any problems."

"The trip was perfect as usual," Alex laughed. "Traveling in your G550 is an unbelievable experience."

"Well, I'm glad you both had a pleasant trip and enjoyed it. I've set up a few things for us while we're down here to mix in a bit of pleasure with business. Contrary to popular opinion, I do like my employees to have a little downtime."

"Thanks for setting up the round of golf," Trucker replied. "Although it's been a while, I'm really looking forward to taking it up tomorrow."

After finishing his cocktail, Mac replied, "As am I, and we can use the opportunity to catch up all the more. How is everything progressing with fast track from a financial standpoint?"

"Things are all falling into place right now," Trucker answered. "We have financial contracts with some key brokerage firms to execute the trades based on our trading plan. The consulting firm we hired has also completed the key software elements we need to assist both our marketing and social media programs."

Mac stood from the bar and strolled over to the railing overlooking the Gulf of Mexico and said, "That's fantastic; I assume everything is on budget too?"

"Yes, the software development costs were a bit more than expected, but we ended up spending less on the brokerage program, so it all balanced out, and we're exactly on budget at this point."

Mac smiled, "That's fantastic; the best news I've heard all week. I really appreciate all the hard and dedicated work you've put into this." He then turned to Alex, "Well, Alex, how about the operational side?"

"Things are going along nicely there, too," Alex replied. "We've deployed all the software we need for the job support for both the social media and stock programs, and we've got all the support we need from Jeff Yanko. He hid the software in the back-up lab, so the current management team can't see it."

Mac clapped his hands and grinned, "After all these years, our plan is finally going to happen, and we can move forward with our key elements in place."

He excused himself to make some calls, telling the two men to make themselves comfortable at the bar and that they would head out in a few hours for dinner. Alex and Trucker poured themselves a drink and settled in on the deck in the warm afternoon sunshine.

• • • •

Later that evening, Mac took Alex and Trucker out to dinner at his favorite restaurant —Louisiana Lagniappe. This restaurant was well-known to the locals and featured fresh fish and Cajun cuisine.

The restaurant was on a quiet portion of the harbor, with boats docked just outside. They arrived just as the sun was setting over the water, and they had a spectacular view of boats coming back from the gulf.

Once seated, Mac ordered his favorite meal — grouper stuffed with crabmeat and topped with beurre blanc sauce. The restaurant usually offered this as a nightly special.

The server knew Mac well and brought a bottle of his favorite wine for the group to share.

Mac opened the conversation once they got started with their meal. "I see that our friend in the Senate had some interesting information to share with the Washington Times. "

"Yes," Alex replied, "I saw that disaster just before we got on the plane."

Looking out of the window and admiring the sunset, Mac replied, "The senator is becoming an increasing problem. I really don't like loose ends, and I think his usefulness to our program is now over."

"I kind of figured you would say that," Alex nodded in agreement. "I was thinking about the same thing on the way down here. "

"Alex," Mac answered, pensive. "I need you to take care of this for me. It needs to be done quickly, and, of course, it needs to look like an accident. I assume you can use your regular guy for this?"

"I'm pretty sure I can get him, but we may have to pay a premium if we need to expedite it."

Mac turned his gaze to Alex. "I don't have a problem with that; your guy has done some quality work for us in the past. Make it happen sooner rather than later. "

Trucker had sat quietly during this exchange, sipping on his drink and listening patiently.

"Trucker, do you have a problem with this?" Mac queried his silence.

Trucker quickly replied, "No, no issue. We will all get what's coming to us in the final analysis."

Mack laughed, "Well, that's an interesting way of looking at things. It certainly simplifies your view on life. "

With that, James Mac had sealed Senator Graben's fate over a brief conversation hundreds of miles away from Washington DC. The group return to mostly small talk and comments about the food and view from the restaurant.

· · · ·

Alex and Trucker woke early the following day and met on the deck. The staff had already set a breakfast buffet up for them, with fresh coffee and juice. The two had just started on the food, admiring the view, when Mac joined them.

Stretching, he said, "Good morning, gentlemen. I hope you're finding everything enjoyable for breakfast."

"You really can't beat this view for breakfast!" Alex replied.

Mac laughed. "Why do you think I moved here? I do this every day."

"I wouldn't have any trouble getting used to this," Trucker added.

Mack nodded in agreement. "While I've got you out here, Trucker, I wanted you to take me through the stock manipulation plan and give me a brief status update."

Trucker knew this would be one of the main conversation topics on the trip and was prepared to speak about it. He had also prepared a report that he brought with him to summarize.

"Everything is on track to date," he began. "We have accounts and contracts with multiple brokerage houses that no one can trace back to us. We also have initial buying and selling plans that we can execute based on expected scenarios during the election campaign."

He continued as Mac sat next to them and started on the breakfast food. "We will time the buying and selling campaigns against major policy speeches the president gives to drive the market in the opposite direction. Every time he makes a promise about the economy, we will do our best to drive economic activity the exact opposite way. It won't take long for him to look like a fool."

Mac laughed and replied, "That's fantastic. Nothing would make me happier than to shame him. How does the quantum lab play into all this?"

Trucker was eager to reply, "This is where the magic begins. We will feed our trading plan and daily results into the quantum lab, where our trading simulator is running. The simulator will evaluate our buying and selling options and optimize our plan to make sure we are getting the results we want. It would take months to run these simulations without the quantum lab and would be too slow to get the feedback we need to drive the results."

Mac then questioned, "Are we sure this is going to work?"

"Based on our initial simulations and test buys, we think our campaigns will be over ninety percent successful. So, we have a high level of confidence that we can drive whatever result we're looking for."

"This is even better than I hoped," Mac replied. "It will be a great tool for us after the campaign."

"What's even better," Trucker added, "is that our model will use deep learning algorithms over time to become even better. After we win the election and get our guy in there, we can take this to the next level to drive whatever type of economic activity we want."

"That's the kind of forward-thinking I'm after," Mac nodded.

Trucker quickly added, "I've detailed all the results of our initial trading tests and the output of the model for you in a report. It's in your encrypted folder with the usual password protection."

Mac got up from the table and replied, "Trucker, you've truly done some outstanding work on this." He turned to Alex. "And I appreciate the work you've done with the brokerage houses, Alex, to get this off the ground. If you'll excuse me, I have a couple of things to do before we head out to the golf course."

With that, Mac went inside, and Trucker and Alex took the time to finish their breakfast and enjoy the Florida sunshine.

. . . .

Mac practiced a few short putts, struggling. "Alex," he began, "now that Trucker has taken me through the stock manipulation plan, can you bring me up to date on our social media strategy?"

Alex replied, "Of course. I also created a report, but I will give you the high level of what we've done so far."

Mac never took part in social media, but he understood its importance, particularly in the scope of a presidential campaign.

"Since we had such outstanding success with the stock trading model, we developed a variant of it for social media positioning," Alex explained. "Although the data points are different, we could reuse some deep learning algorithms so that, based on our social media posting, we could quickly drive public sentiment in the direction we want."

Mac replied, "That's a stroke of genius. I'm glad we didn't have to start over from scratch with this model."

Alex nodded. "We will target both candidates with the usual social media smear campaign and then feed those results back into the model to see where it's most effective. We're not very concerned about the democratic candidate, but Witte is firmly entrenched as the incumbent and has a significant advantage at this point."

He quickly pressed on now that he was on a roll. "The power of our model is a neural network that learns quickly and gives us almost instantaneous feedback on our social media posts. We control tens of thousands of bot accounts that cannot be traced back to us and will flood social media with whatever sentiment we desire. You will see the approval ratings of both candidates plummet once the model completes several learning cycles."

"I'm guessing the quantum lab's speed is also key to this, too?"

"Yes, without it, we can't process the data fast enough to implement feedback in the process loop. With the results we're getting now, we can drive public sentiment in almost real-time."

Mac smiled. "With the combination of our market manipulation and social media models, the other two candidates won't stand a chance."

Alex returned the grin, then finished the conversation with, "Also, we will fold the simulation results into our legitimate advertising to create a perfect storm for our candidate. We can even decide on the margin of victory we want to achieve."

"Alex," Mac clapped a hand on his shoulder, "this is all fantastic. I'm so glad that both of you came down here to share these results with me. Everything has exceeded my wildest expectations."

Satisfied from what he had heard from both Alex and Trucker, Mac prepared to tee-off. Everything was on track for the election.

Even though Alex and Trucker were not regular golfers, they enjoyed their time out on the course, taking the opportunity to have a few cocktails. They headed into the clubhouse to grab some lunch after the round, chatting and laughing about the day, including some agonizing short puts Mac had missed. He had a pretty excellent sense of humor about it, but Alex knew it must have really bothered him deep down.

After they finished golf, it was time for Alex and Trucker to fly home. They listened as Mac summed up his feelings about the trip.

"Gentlemen, I want to thank you so much for coming down here and updating me on the progress of fast track. All the results you have presented me have wildly exceeded my expectations. I'm truly grateful for all the hard work you've done, and I put something in both your accounts to show my appreciation. We've still got lots of work to do, but we're off to a brilliant start."

Mac's brief speech relieved and delighted both Alex and Trucker. All three lifted their glasses and toasted to their organization's success.

Once again, Mac cut things short. "I'd love to stay and have another drink with you guys, but I have to attend another appointment. I sent the limo to take you back to the airport whenever you are done. Hopefully, we will have the opportunity to do this again soon. I'll wait to hear from both of you for further updates."

Mac headed into his beach house, leaving Alex and Trucker to finish off their lunch as they waited for the limousine to arrive.

• • • •

On the plane back home, Alex was curious to know Trucker's feelings about the operation. This was out of character for him since he usually didn't care about coworkers' feelings on a particular project.

Still, for some reason, he felt compelled to ask. "I realize this is not a typical project you have worked on in the past. Are you comfortable with all this?"

Trucker did not need any time to think about his reply. "I've worked on so many projects over the years where I didn't get anything out of it. In this case, it's a steady gig, and I'm getting well paid. I guess I'm kind of jaded, but I really don't care about the consequences. The longer I have worked in my career, the more I really care about what's in it for me!"

Brun laughed, "I'm glad I asked. I feel exactly the same!"

They continued the journey, now in a lighter mood than before they had set off, laughing and taking advantage of the free drinks on Mac's plane.

With all the key elements in place, fast track was ready to move onto the next phase that would change the course of history.

Chapter 9 Operation in the Desert

The plan was for Jack and Jeffers to fly out to Las Vegas the day before the conference, giving them plenty of time to check in.

After an uneventful, direct flight, they picked up a rental and headed toward Caesars Palace, where the conference was taking place and where they'd be staying. Even though the mission was heavy on both their minds, they were still a little excited about getting out of town and spending some time in Las Vegas.

Once they got to the hotel, they went to the registration desk for the conference and picked up their badges for the next day. Everything was proceeding as expected.

Since they had nothing planned for the rest of the day, Jack and Jeffers spent some time wandering around, checking out the shops and all the interesting things you can only find at Caesars.

Jack also took the time to pick up something for Lucy. He always liked to bring something back, even if it was something small. It had become a bit of a tradition with Jack and Lucy; she was always excited to get something from wherever Jack had traveled to.

After they killed some time wandering around Caesars Palace, Jack and Jeffers headed to their own rooms to go over their plans for the operation.

Jeffers went through his equipment checklist to make sure he had everything and reviewed his contingency plans in case anything went wrong with any step of the mission. He had trained for this type of operation; his planning resulted from years of experience.

Jack also spent some time reviewing his code and practicing the installation operation he would perform in the lab. He had a great deal of experience with this type of work and knew that practice and testing were critical factors for success. Jack really wanted to take his time during this testing and review, so he ordered room service and continued his work into the evening.

. . . .

The next day, Jack and Jeffers attended the conference — The World Congress in Computer Science, Computer Engineering, & Applied Computing. With everything they planned for the operation, it was difficult for them to keep their minds on the event, though with a jam-packed agenda, time passed quickly.

They later met for dinner to discuss any last-minute details. They decide to eat at the hotel restaurant since it was so convenient.

Jeffers began up the conversation. "So, Jack, do you think the software is all ready to go?"

"Yes," Jack replied, "I have practiced the install procedure several times, and I'm satisfied that I shouldn't run into any issues. But since this is software, you're never really sure until you try it for real."

Jeffers laughed, "That's why I've stayed away from software and IT my entire career!"

"How about your plan to breach the base?" Jack asked.

"All good to go. I packed a few extra items to take with us for contingencies. Thankfully, this is not my first rodeo!"

"That's why I'm not worried since you're handling all of it," Jack nodded. "I assume that, since everything is ready, we just need to meet up tomorrow evening in the lobby at eight?"

"Yes," Jeffers agreed, "that should give us plenty of time to get to the airport and meet Hankins." Frank Hankins was the chopper pilot.

"Sounds good."

"You'll get a kick out of meeting Frank. He's really out there, but I assure you he is one hell of a pilot."

"Once again, I'm glad you've planned all that part of the mission," Jack smiled.

They went about ordering their food for dinner. Although done discussing the mission, it weighed heavily on their minds for the rest of that evening.

· · · ·

Jack and Jeffers woke the next morning to attend the second day of the conference. They wanted to go to as many sessions as they could, though Jack could not pay any attention to them, as he was thinking about the mission that evening. Now that they were so close, time seemed to crawl by. Finally, Jack headed back to his room before meeting up with Jeffers. He was tired enough to get in a brief nap and headed down to the lobby cafe to grab a quick sandwich.

While finishing up, Jack spotted Jeffers leaving the elevator. He quickly paid his bill and joined him.

"Ready to go?" Jeffers asked when he approached.

"As ready as I'll ever be," Jack nervously laughed.

They picked up their gear and left for the rental car, driving to McCarran airport to pick up their charter helicopter flight. Using the cover of taking a trip to Lake Mead and Hoover dam at sunset, they would instead fly to the air force base under radar cover and sneak on for Jack to install his logging software.

Once at the airport, they entered a special access code to take them to the remote hangar and the helicopter charter. They pulled up to see a shabby-looking man who looked like he'd just stumbled out of a bar pop out of the helicopter.

"Hey, are you Jack Brown?" the man yelled.

"Yeah, I am, unfortunately," said Jack.

The man grinned, "Damn glad to meet you, Jack; I'm Frank Hankins."

Jeffers had explained to Jack over dinner the previous night that Hankins was a former army chopper pilot the agency routinely used on covert missions; they basically owned him after a charter job he took on years ago in Columbus, Ohio, to fly some signage for the State football game. Later that evening, Hankins was at a party that had gotten out of control, culminating in Hankins flying some scantily clad women in a late-night flight, where he landed in Ohio Stadium. Needless to say, campus police and the FAA were none too happy about it. The agency sent some people to clean up the mess, and Hankins had been at their beck and call for charter work ever since.

Though a bit of a mess personally, Jack learned that Frank was one hell of a chopper pilot. He was a decorated Iraq war veteran and could fly any chopper under any conditions. Jeffers swore by him and had told Jack several stories about how Hankins had pulled him out of tight spots many times.

The chopper sat just outside the hanger, positioned to take off right away.

Hankins bellowed out to Jack and Jeffers, "Throw your stuff in and make yourselves comfortable; we can get going whenever you're ready."

Jack wasn't sure whether Hankins was completely sane or sober based on his appearance, but he grabbed his gear and jumped into the chopper. Jeffers quickly followed, and they buttoned up for the flight.

. . . .

Once the helicopter got to Lake Mead, Hankins contacted air traffic control and told them he was about to land.

Hankins began the descent into the landing zone, but once near the ground, he proceeded in a vertical terrain pattern so that air traffic control couldn't track him with radar. This was a key aspect of the plan, looking like the helicopter had landed and will be there while performing the rest of the operation.

Though Jack was concerned about Hankins's pilot skills, he quickly showed that he was more than capable and had done this many times before. Jack could tell he actually enjoyed this part of the flight and got some kind of rush out of it.

Hankins told Jack and Jeffers that they would be at the landing zone within a couple of minutes. Soon after, he made his approach to an open area at the base of a small mountain. He had picked it since it would help mask them from the nearby air force base radar and the nearest spot they could land without being detected.

Once on the ground, Jeffers took control and unloaded the equipment they would need to breach the outer base's security, including night vision goggles so they could see better during their hike through the desert. In the meantime, Hankins shut down the helicopter to make sure they wouldn't make any more noise or commotion than necessary. Jack and Jeffers quickly packed up for their hike and made their way toward the base.

After about twenty minutes, they could see the air force base and the outer perimeter fence. They approached, and Jeffers shorted the electric, using a dead animal he'd found in the woods as cover. The plan was they would go back in the bush and hide and wait for the guards to come and check out the incident.

Within just a couple of minutes, a Humvee drove to the fence, and a couple of guards got out and looked around. As per the plan, they quickly found the animal and surmised that it had caused the short. They then took the fence offline so a maintenance crew could make repairs first thing in the morning.

This was Jack and Jeffers's opportunity to breach the base undetected.

Jeffers had packed a portable folding ladder, allowing them to quickly climb over the fence without touching it. Once on the other side, Jeffers pulled the ladder back over, folded it, and hid it in under some brush. He then marked the spot so they could quickly return to it on their way out.

After scaling the fence, Jeffers led the way to the building that contained the backup quantum lab. It turned out to be a short distance, as Jeffers's plan crossed at the closest point from the outer fence to the lab. As they drew close, Jack removed the outer jumpsuit he wore, revealing his civilian clothes.

Since Jack had legitimate credentials to enter the lab, the first and most dangerous part of the mission was over. As the technical director of this project, he had full access to the facility. If spotted, Jack knew most of the staff, and they would not question his presence. He preferred not to meet anyone once he entered the building, but he was reasonably confident that no staff would be in the lab at this time of the evening.

Jack's only concern was to alter the video that tracked the hallways to the lab entrance, though he had made a plan for it.

While Jack was in the lab, Jeffers found a spot where he could hide and monitor the building's entrance, alerting Jack if he spotted anyone.

· · · ·

Once Jack entered the building housing the lab, he quickly made his way to the entrance and swiped his access card. As he had calculated, no one was in the building, and everything was silent. Up to this point, the plan was working as expected.

Once in the lab, everything was exactly as it was the last time he had been there. Jack made his way to one of the system consoles and quickly set up to make his modifications.

He plugged in the USB drive containing all the software patches for the new logging software. He ran several set-up scripts that would install the software and place any of the necessary drivers in the correct directories. The set-up itself only took a couple of minutes, so Jack took his time to make sure everything was in place, performing a quick smoke test to ensure the software was running correctly.

Jack then kicked off a job that would splice the entry logs into the lab to make it look like he was never there. He also double-checked his work to make sure it would completely cover his tracks. As part of this job, he calculated his exit time so the software would erase that portion of the video. Once he completed the final test, he set his watch timer to 120 seconds, just enough time to exit the lab and cover his tracks.

He quickly packed up the bag he had brought and made his way out of the lab to meet up with Jeffers. They both quickly made their way back to the fence to exit the base and meet up with Hankins.

Just before they set off, Jeffers spotted a guard patrol making a pass. They quickly hid out of sight, and after a few minutes, the guard truck moved on, and they could finally make their way to the fence.

They quickly scaled the barrier, put on their night vision goggles, and returned to the small mountain, where the helicopter waited.

. . . .

Hankins spotted Jack and Jeffers nearing the helicopter and began his startup procedure. It took just a couple of minutes for the two of them to jog the final yards and hop in. Soon, they were airborne, and Hankins executed his terrain-following path back to Lake Mead.

Once underway, Hankins shouted back to Jack and Jeffers, "How did everything go?"

"I can't believe it, but everything went as planned," Jack replied. "We really didn't encounter anything unexpected at all."

Jeffers then chimed in, "Yeah, it's hard to believe with all the things that could've gone wrong, nothing did."

Hankins yelled back at them, "That's great to hear. Nothing better than a happy customer!"

He returned his concentration back to the flight and terrain following. Within just a few minutes, they had landed at a designated spot at Lake Mead.

All three took a deep breath, needing a few minutes to decompress before taking the flight back to McCarran airport in Las Vegas.

Jack reflected on the evening's events, his mind running with the potential consequences if someone found out about the mission.

Jeffers spotted a concerned look on Jack's face. "Jack, don't stress out over this; you've done the right thing here. Even though this operation is well out of the norm for you, we really need to find out what's going on and who is behind it."

Surprised by Jeffers's comments, Jack replied, "Thanks; you read my mind! I was just thinking about all the things that could go wrong after this. But you're right; we really didn't have a choice."

"No problem," Jeffers smiled. "I've been in this situation more times than I care to admit."

That calmed Jack down and allowed him to sit back and relax for the rest of the flight. Within just a few minutes, they arrived back at the hangar at McCarran airport, thanking Hankins for the great work he had done that evening. Since it was getting late, Jack and Jeffers wasted no time in grabbing their gear from the helicopter and packing up the rental.

. . . .

Jack and Jeffers met up in the lobby at five the following morning for their early flight back to DC. They had both already grabbed coffee and were ready to leave for the airport, quickly getting their things and heading to get into the rental car for the drive back. Since it was a short drive to the airport and there was no traffic at that time in the morning, the trip went by quickly. Neither had much to say since it was so early and they were both exhausted from the night before.

Once at the airport and after returning the rental, they realized they had plenty of extra time and stopped for breakfast.

After they had sat down and placed their order, Jack opened the conversation with, "I don't know about you, but I'm really looking forward to getting back home."

"Yeah, me too," Jeffers replied. "After all these years of travel, it wears on me even more now."

Jack laughed, "Yeah, I'm not really wired for business travel. I just don't sleep very well when I'm on the road; I guess I'm just a homeboy. "

"Nothing wrong with that," Jeffers shrugged.

"True. By the way," Jack added, "I did a status check on the software installed yesterday, and it seems to work."

Jeffers replied, sipping his coffee, "That's great. Hopefully, we can now make some sense out of this mess."

"Yeah, I am eager to get together with Frank and look through some of this data."

"I'm pretty sure once you look at it, you'll be glad we came out here," Jeffers smiled.

Jack agreed, and they went about finishing up their breakfast, shortly leaving to catch the flight home.

Chapter 10 The Hit on Senator Graben

The first thing Lucy did at work every morning was read the Washington Times. She had developed a powerful method and could scan through the paper in about thirty minutes to make sure it contained nothing she needed to know or pass along for the senator's attention.

While reading the paper on this particular morning, an article leaped off the page, detailing the CIA's quantum computing lab. Lucy was horrified when she saw the way it was written, clearly implying that much of the information came from Senator Graben's office.

Lucy knew the information had not come from her, and she wondered if the senator had somehow inadvertently told someone else, who had then leaked it to the paper. She was just finishing reading when the senator popped into her office on his way in.

He wasted no time and quickly spoke up, "I guess you saw the disaster printed in this morning's Times? I'd like to throttle whoever let that information loose. I can assure you it wasn't me."

Lucy could tell he was in a foul mood and wanted to make his way to his office as fast as possible; this was not the morning to joke with him.

She anticipated that he needed the morning to make a series of phone calls to minimize the damage. With this in mind, she told him she'd get started on clearing his schedule right away.

"Thanks so much, Lucy," Graben replied. "I don't know what I would do without you. I'll buzz you later if I need anything."

He hurried into his office to see what he could do over the phone to clean some of this mess up. Lucy could hear his door slam — something he rarely did. There is no way she would ever want his job with all that pressure. Every day was a balancing act, and everyone had to be very careful about what they said — particularly to the press.

Lucy wondered what type of long-term damage this type of incident could do to the senator. She really had no idea of the desperate trouble he was in.

• • • •

While on the flight home from Florida, Alex called the hitman he had reliably used in the past named Pete Browser. Mac and Alex called him "Paradise Pete" since he always produced such consistent results for them. Browser was an unscrupulous type of hitman who played on all sides, but he was very effective. Alex knew that if he paid top dollar, he could get Browser, and the job will be done right away.

Once the hitman picked up, Alex gave him the proper code word. "Hey, I have a job for you with the usual terms."

"Always happy to help; what date are you looking at?" Browser replied. Alex had already arranged the date with Mac.

"I'm looking to get this done within the next week."

Browser paused for a moment. "I will have to clear some things off my calendar to make that happen. I'm assuming you're able to pay the premium rate for this?"

Alex quickly added, "We are fine with paying the premium rate — just make sure you get it done with no loose ends."

Since Browser had done this so many times, he almost instinctively said, "Absolutely, I will go through the normal detailed protocol and the confirmation. I will expect payment and the normal method in the account you already have on file."

Alex was pleased to hear this and closed out the conversation. "We will pay you for this when we get the usual confirmation from you. If you run into any issues, let us know right away."

"I'll get working on this right away. Make sure you have all the details of my target in the usual location."

"They're already there," Alex said before hanging up. He messaged Mac on a secure line, saying everything was in order and ready to go with the job. Alex had done enough of these that he no longer thought about the killing — he just treated it like the next task and marked it complete in a project plan.

· · · ·

Right after Browser hung up the phone, he opened a file in a secure location and used a custom encryption method to decode the details.

Though the file revealed that he would eliminate a United States senator, it did not faze him. Pete had been doing this long enough and had eliminated enough high-profile targets that he simply thought of this as the next job.

He was also experienced enough to know that since this was a high-profile target, he would have to be careful to ensure it looked like an accident and that he could cover his trail entirely.

Browser had become an expert at planning travel for these types of jobs and knew how to find inconspicuous places to rent through Airbnb, booking them under a fake credit card he'd been using for a while.

He could also advance-ship some supplies to an Amazon unit so that he had everything he needed already on-site; he only had to pick it up.

Browser picked up the supplies after arriving in DC and headed straight to his rental Airbnb unit, meticulously preparing everything for this job as soon as he got there.

Over time, Browser had developed an exact methodology for preparing for these jobs, a sort of project plan he followed each time he went out on. The first step was to come up with a general plan. In this case, he would use a bomb to blow the tires on the senator's limousine at the exact moment he was crossing the bridge over the Potomac River.

To ensure that anyone in the limousine would not survive, Browser would also place a small vial of poison gas inside that would shatter when the explosion occurred. This gas would only be traceable in the case of an autopsy, but there was a little chance of this with the car crash covering the hit.

The next step in the process was to observe the senator's movements to confirm that he followed a daily routine. Browser would use that to his advantage to guarantee he was in place and could activate the explosives when the car crossed the bridge. He would typically observe subjects for at least two days to make sure they would repeat the pattern and maximize his chances of success.

In this case, Browser confirmed that Senator Graben took the same route every day and found just the spot to duplicate the timing he needed for the hit.

Browser decided to do a complete practice run on the third day to confirm everything was in place. This was the final step in his plan to ensure everything would go flawlessly — which it did.

He prepared to execute the job on the fourth day. He was ready to pull the trigger.

. . . .

During the morning of the job, Browser went about constructing the bomb. During the day, he would place it under the car once it was parked in the garage. He had previously worked out a method to gain access to it, so he could quickly slip in and place the bomb without being noticed.

Browser had learned long ago that it was best to build the bomb at the very last minute since it was not a particularly good thing to have a live explosive device around for days at a time for a job. Since he had practiced this many times, the construction went without a hitch, and he parked his rental car in the area where he needed to plant the bomb.

He could easily plant the bomb during noon, despite the substantial traffic around the senator's parked limousine. The bomb was small and compact, and Browser had devised a method where he only needed to stroll by the car, quickly duck under, and plant it in about thirty seconds.

Once the bomb was in place, Browser had plenty of time to tie up any loose ends back at his rental condo. He started a timer to go off one hour before the senator's scheduled commute time. Browser had observed the senator head out within fifteen to thirty minutes around the same time every single day. He was hoping this trend would continue and nothing would derail the plan.

Once the appointed time went off on his timer, Browser packed up everything he needed and proceeded to the observation point. He sat and waited for about fifteen minutes before spotting the senator's limousine approaching the bridge. Just as the vehicle moved forward, Browser pressed the detonation button, and the bomb went off as expected.

Right on schedule, the limousine pulled a hard left and plummeted over the railing into the river. Being in the middle of rush hour, it was complete chaos on the bridge, and several other cars crashed into each other due to the confusion.

Browser patiently waited for a good twenty minutes to ensure that nobody escaped from the limousine to the river's surface. He saw the EMT services arrive and confirm that they did not see any survivors. Soon after, helicopters and other emergency services came to the scene and attempted a dive in the river to look for any survivors.

At this point, Browser had seen enough and would get the final confirmation by watching the local news.

. . . .

Browser left the scene and returned to his rental condo, careful to meticulously clean it before leaving, including wiping off any possible prints. He had learned over the years to be exceptionally cautious and take his time to get every detail just right.

While cleaning up, Browser turned on the TV to monitor the news reports and saw the divers pulling a body out of the Potomac River. Once he had this level of confirmation, he called Brun to confirm that his job had been completed.

Brun stated that the payment had been put into his account and would close off this job. Browser hung up and turned his efforts into finishing the cleanup so that he can quickly and quietly get out of town.

. . . .

After Alex heard from Browser, he gave Mac a call to let him know that everything was completed. Mac requested him to set up a meeting during the funeral with himself, Alex, and Michael Graham. They were all expected at the funeral anyway and would like to take the opportunity to catch up on the progress of fast track since they last met.

Chapter 11 The Graben Funeral

Senator Graben had been in office for five consecutive terms. He was very popular in Ohio and showed no signs of slowing down. He frequently traveled back and forth between his hometown in Cleveland, Ohio, and Washington DC and kept in regular touch with his constituents back home.

He was also popular on both sides of the aisle. Despite being a bit of a lush and womanizer, Graben had a very likable personality and a way of getting things done, even when things became contentious in Congress. Graben was a conservative republican, but he had a way of reaching out to the other side and finding common ground on complex issues. He was a rare politician and not the prototype of the current day and age.

Serving on many prestigious committees during his tenure in the Senate, Graben's most recent appointment was chair of the Senate Intelligence Committee. His colleges saw this as his crowning achievement. Graben also sponsored some meaningful legislation in his career. Everyone knew him for his bipartisanship and his practical sense of governing.

With his popularity and term length in the Senate, the funeral's attendee list was long and distinguished. This was not a typical political funeral, where most people were there because they had to be. Most attendees truly cared about the senator and had heartfelt grief from his loss. Due to the large expected crowd at the funeral, the church service was small — limited to family only, with Arlington National Cemetery as the venue for the large-scale ceremony.

Jack and Lucy both expected a large turnout for the graveside service, but the number of attendees really surprised them. The size and scale of Graben's funeral was something more fitting for a head of state than a member of Congress. A considerable press contingent also attended the proceedings but kept their distance during the actual service out of respect. A colossal security contingent was also in place due to the number of high-ranking officials attending.

• • • •

Senator Graben's staff went to a great deal of trouble to set up the funeral site as a really moving tribute to him. The place had incredible bouquets of flowers and wreaths decorated with red and white bows, mixing well with the American flag covering his casket. Small American flags also decorated each row of chairs where guests were seated. A large picture of the senator lay behind the casket, adorned with a black lace cloth.

Before the ceremony began, a beautiful collection of songs from some of the most well-known recording artists in the industry emitted. The music also included a moving performance from Yo-Yo Ma. With help from the White House, the senator's staff truly made this an extraordinary event.

The head of the Washington archdiocese of the Catholic Church proceeded over the service. Senator Graben was a devout Catholic and had known the bishop for many years, and his family had deep roots within the Catholic Church.

After the bishop opened the service and said a brief prayer, President Witte took to the podium. The president and Senator Graben had been lifelong friends. His speech praised the senator's life in many of the bipartisan efforts he had spearheaded over such a long and distinguished career. He also praised him for the outstanding representation he gave the great state of Ohio over many years. Both President Witte and Graben were Ohio natives, and they had a great affection for the state.

Finally, the president closed his eulogy with a heartfelt goodbye to his dear friend. His speech deeply moved all the people in attendance; the president was a brilliant orator and knew how to hit emotional high spots and drive the message home.

Once his speech had concluded, the bishop presided over the rest of the funeral, with *Amazing Grace* on the bagpipes. There truly were no dry eyes in the audience that day.

. . . .

After the service ended, most dignitaries mingled with the crowd to catch up with old friends. Jack and Lucy were getting ready to leave for the wake at the local pub when Jack saw the president wave at him. He was chatting with some ranking members of the Senate, seemingly relieved that the service had concluded

Though not close, Jack had met President Witte several times, and he was also from Ohio. They shared a sort of Buckeye bond that many people from Ohio know well. Jack and Lucy waited patiently for the president to make his way over to them.

"Hello, Jack!" bellowed President Witte. "I haven't seen you since the big game in Columbus, OH!"

"IO!" Jack replied, requiring no explanation for anyone who's an Ohio State football fan.

The president was quick to say to Lucy, "I'm very sorry for your loss. We all loved Senator Graben; I will sorely miss his work."

"Thank you so much; that means so much to me that you came here and spoke," Lucy sniffed.

"Of course, he was like a brother to me. I will really miss him," he added, choking up himself. He then quickly followed up with, "I'm sorry I can't stay and talk longer, but my wife is giving me that look, so I had better get her out of here."

Lucy chuckled, "I understand completely; I have been giving Jack that look for the last twenty minutes!"

President Witte then said, "God bless both of you, and I hope you can get some peace and healing after this ceremony. Jack, I also want to set up a meeting with you soon. Some people on my staff want to see if they can leverage your project, and we need your expertise."

"Of course, I'd be happy to help," Jack quickly replied.

The president and his security detail slowly made their way through the sizeable crowd and to their car.

• • • •

While walking out, Jack noticed Alex Brun, James Mac, and Michael Graham talking. Jack only vaguely knew of James Mac and next to nothing about Graham, apart from his public persona. He was a late entry in the presidential race and running as an independent. He had recently started gaining some traction and was now getting a lot of press coverage. A seasoned politician, Graham had spent several terms in the US Senate representing the state of Minnesota. The public viewed Graham as more of a moderate, and he'd spent a lot of time in his career building bipartisan coalitions.

Something had changed with Graham over the last few years, and he had become a much more aggressive politician. He had made a name for himself, exposing graft and corruption in the Senate. Many people liked him for this, but it made him very unpopular with his colleagues, using exposure to enhance his own career and image.

While Jack and Lucy made their way toward their limousine, Jack noticed Jeff Yanko had joined the conversation. The group seemed to be very friendly with Yanko, further deepening Jack's suspicions that his boss had involved himself in whatever was going on with the quantum lab.

· · · ·

After the funeral, Michael Graham, Alex Brun, and James Mac engaged in light conversation about their impressions of the funeral. Jeff Yanko briefly joined and took part in the discussion, though he didn't stay long, merely stopping by to say hello. Yanko would talk to them later; this was not the best venue to discuss business with them. After just a few minutes, he left the group, and the other three got into a limousine to head to the wake in Georgetown.

The tone of conversation changed quickly once on the road; they no longer had to be careful about what they were saying in public.

James Mac opened the conversation. "Well, with this job done lit eaves us one less complication as we near the election. Alex, I'm glad your connection could get this job done so quickly and make it look like an accident. I was getting really uneasy with how loose the senator was getting with sensitive information."

Alex replied, "I'm also relieved to get this job behind us. The information he had could've really hurt us; I'm glad it ties up a loose end."

Michael Graham then chimed into the conversation. "I hear all is going well with the lab at this point in time and that things are rapidly progressing."

"Yes, things are moving fantastically well, and we are really ramping up production," Alex answered. "We will be ready when the election enters the next phase. We will make sure you will have the easiest election campaign in history. With what we have planned, you will win by a landslide."

Mac laughed, adding, "I can't wait to see the look on Witte's face as all these calamities hurtle at him one after the other. He doesn't stand a chance with what we have planned. We also have a hefty dose queued up for the other side. It will be fun to watch it unfold."

"None of these guys will know what hit them!" Alex chuckled. "They will be so far back on their heels that the campaign will be ours in no time."

"Once we get you in there, Grammy, that's when the real magic will happen," Mac grinned. "We can finally move our plan into full motion."

Michael Graham closed things off. "It's great when a plan falls together. At last, we can activate all those forces we have been building and putting in place all these years."

Mac reached over to the middle of the limousine and opened a bottle of champagne the driver had put on ice. He poured each of them a glass, and they toasted to their successful operation.

Several minutes later, the limousine arrived at the Irish pub in Georgetown, where the wake was held. They would change their tone and demeanor and dutifully pay their respects to the friends, family, and colleagues of the senator they had just killed. They had done this so many times over the past few years that they didn't need to think twice about it.

• • • •

After the conversation with President Witte, Jack and Lucy made their way to the limousine to attend the wake that Senator Graben's staff had scheduled. Neither had much to say on the ride there since they were both still pretty shaken by everything that had happened.

They arrived and entered a large private room at the back that the staff had reserved for the wake. Even though the space was fairly large, Senator Graben's friends and family packed it full. Jack and Lucy were somewhat hesitant about going to the event due to their mental states.

This was a traditional wake with lots of food and drinks and an open bar, though neither Jack nor Lucy felt like having one and began working their way through the crowd, talking to all the familiar faces. Despite being apprehensive about going to the wake, they felt a little more at ease after talking to a few of their friends, appreciating their terrific stories about Senator Graben.

After about thirty minutes of working their way through the crowd, Jack looked over at Lucy and could tell she was getting exhausted. Ever since he walked through the door, he had been thinking about leaving the private room and going up to the public portion to have a quiet dinner with Lucy.

She thought that was a great idea when he decided to ask her, and they both made their way out, asking the bartender about getting a table for dinner.

. . . .

The pub the wake was held at was also one of Lucy's and Jack's favorite places, but even with her newfound push to go out more often together, they had not been to this place in quite some time.

There was a ten or fifteen-minute wait for a table, so Jack and Lucy decided to stay at the bar and have a drink before dinner. It had been a long and stressful day, and they hoped it would help them relax a little.

Once they were seated and had ordered, Jack began to speak. "How are you doing, Lucy?"

Lucy smiled, "A little raw at this point. I really don't know what to think. All this happened so quickly; I feel like things are really coming at me a little too fast. "

Jack held her hand. "I understand completely. I'm so sorry you had to go through all this. I realize how difficult it must be. Maybe you should think about taking some time off to let things settle down a bit. "

"You'll never know how much your love and support mean to me," Lucy beamed. "I really mean that. I have been thinking about taking a break, actually, and going back to Ohio to visit the family until things calm down here."

"I think that's a great idea," Jack replied. "I was even going to suggest that to you. I think your family can really help you out right now, and having some distance between you and DC would really help."

"I'll start looking at flights and making the arrangements," Lucy nodded. "I'll also talk to the office and let them know I'm going to be taking some time off." She paused briefly. "How about you? How are things going with the lab?"

Jack sighed. "I'm still very uneasy with things. I'm uncertain about the extent of the tampering, but I've made efforts to put monitoring in place so we can get some data and see what's going on."

He paused, a strange look appearing on his face, and continued, "I also have a confession to make: my recent trip to Las Vegas was just not a trip to the usual nerd convention. I've moved ahead with the plan to put some software in the lab so I can track what is going on with nobody else knowing."

Lucy laughed and replied, "That doesn't surprise me at all. You seemed pretty nervous about the trip. I figured there was something else going on."

"I'm sorry I didn't tell you, but I just didn't want you to worry. I hope this plan I put in place will help me figure stuff out."

"Were you careful to cover your tracks?" Lucy asked.

"Yes, I hope so," Jack nodded. "I got a lot of help from Jeffers, who went with me on the trip, and I'm ninety-nine percent certain that no one knew we were even at the backup lab."

"That's good; I'm worried that somehow the senator's death relates to this mess. This is another reason I want to go to Ohio. I'm afraid of what we have exactly become involved in."

With a concerned look on his face, Jack said, "I'm anxious about that too. I would desperately like to get out of this situation, but we have to wait for the right time."

He continued, "Whatever is going on here is important enough for me to really find out. I don't think I can just bail without getting some data from this. I'm afraid that the size and scope of this operation might have unbelievable implications for our country. I just can't walk away."

"I think you're doing the right thing," Lucy replied, squeezing his hand. "Trying to get some data out of this thing and not implicate yourself in any way is the right plan. Once you figure out what's going on, you can perhaps find someone to help you stop it. "

"I'm glad you agree. I think we need to make long-term plans to get ourselves out of this mess. I don't think it's going to go away anytime soon," Jack replied.

The magnitude of this conversation drained whatever energy they had left. They ate quickly, wanting to get home as soon as possible.

They both knew that, based on today's events, their lives would change forever.

Chapter 12 The Meeting with President Witte

S oon after Senator Graben's funeral, Jack received an invitation by way of the director's office to go to a meeting at the White House to brief the president on the progress of the quantum computing project.

He shot an email to Jeff Yanko to ask about the event's protocol. Yanko quickly responded, noting that only Jack would be going to the meeting as the sole representative of the briefing agency. This response surprised Jack, and in the back of his mind, he thought the director and Jeff were probably pissed that the invitation did not include them.

In his email response, Yanko also said he had all the agency resources at his disposal; they wanted this briefing to go well for the president. Jack had a sinking feeling in his stomach, what with the pressure of this meeting and the agency director's and his boss's expectations.

After reading the email, Jack got down to business. He organized the presentation and contacted various people in the agency to help him pull resources for it. He wanted to complete it well before the deadline, so there would be ample time for review.

. . . .

Jack had about one week to prepare for the meeting at the White House. It was not a particularly demanding assignment to put this briefing together for the president and a few select cabinet members. Still, it had the additional pressure of pleasing the president, the director, and his boss.

On the plus side, since it was such a high visibility briefing, Jack had no problem getting resources or putting any of the materials together. Knowing he could ask and anyone would drop whatever they were doing to help made completing this type of assignment much more manageable.

The team put the presentation together very quickly and went through a couple of preview cycles with the director and Jack's boss. He beat the deadline, including the package of booklets. Now all he had to do was wait for the big day.

. . . .

Finally, the meeting day had arrived, and Jack drove his car to the White House. The guard carefully checked Jack's credentials and double-checked that he was on the president's agenda that morning. The gate's security was impressive; it would take an unbelievable amount of force to penetrate.

After passing through initial security, Jack finally made his way to the Oval Office's waiting area. He didn't consider himself a close friend with President Witte, but he wasn't nervous, as he did know him reasonably well from his days back in Ohio.

After waiting about ten or fifteen minutes, the president's receptionist told Jack they were ready for him. Despite being familiar with the President, it was still a big thrill to go into the Oval Office. Once the door was opened for him, he saw President Witte sitting at the resolute desk, finishing up some paperwork. The secretary of defense, the chief of homeland security, and the president's chief of staff were sat on couches and nodded at Jack as he entered.

"Hi, Jack, and welcome to the Oval Office!" he said jovially once he spotted him. "Thank you for being willing to share your project's progress with me."

"Thanks," Jack grinned. "It's quite a thrill to be here; I'm eager to take you through what we've been working on."

President Witte made a waving motion for him to make his way over to a set of couches to start going through the briefing. The agency had supplied hard copies for all participants in the meeting, which the president's aide now distributed.

The president kicked off the meeting by introducing Jack to the rest of the group. He mentioned they knew each other from their past in Ohio; President Witte never missed an opportunity to say that Jack was also a big Buckeye fan.

After completing the introductions, Jack started going through the briefing. He had carried out many presentations over his career. He got to be pretty good at it, especially developing the right pace and tone.

The handouts included all the details of each slide Jack described. He could read the crowd; they seemed to absorb the content, not disinterested in what he was saying. Some participants had a few questions along the way, mainly drilling down into more detail on the included charts.

There were just a few more questions from the president's chief of staff when the briefing ended, primarily to clarify some of the presentation's key points. The president thanked Jack for his presentation once he had answered all the questions, commenting on how impressed he was with the agency's work with the quantum computing lab.

President Witte dismissed everyone from his office at that point but asked Jack to stick around for a few minutes.

"Jack," he began, "I wanted to thank you again for coming over and giving this a personal touch. I needed more details on this project. I'm so impressed with what you are doing."

"Thank you so much, Mr. President," Jack replied. "I appreciate the opportunity to present the work my team is doing here."

Present Witte then asked, "Jack, is there anything going on...off the books with this project that you would like to tell me about? Anything you would've been uncomfortable saying in front of the group?"

Jack felt his heart race a little and considered his reply. "Nothing out of the ordinary to report. Just the usual trials and tribulations of trying to get a new technology as complex as this one to cooperate."

"Well, if there is ever anything you feel you need to share with me, feel free to reach out. I will instruct my assistant to give you my personal contact method."

Jack was relieved by the president's reply and said, "Thank you so much, Mr. President. I will be certain to contact you if anything comes up."

"I also wanted you to stay behind to ask you how Lucy was doing. I imagine this is a very rough time for her," the president stated with a look of genuine concern.

A slightly pained look on his face, Jack replied, "I think she's doing as well as she can, but you're right — this situation has been rough on her. I wouldn't be surprised if she looked for another job at this point. I think the pain is just too great for her right now."

"Well, we would be sorry to lose her on Capitol Hill," the president replied. "But I completely understand. I wish the best for you both."

That ended the conversation between the two, and Jack made his way out to the receptionist. She had a package waiting for him and instructions on how to personally contact the president. Though Jack had not been nervous during the presentation, he felt like a weight had been lifted off his shoulders and was eager to make his way out of the White House and back home.

· · · · ·

Soon after the meeting with President Witte, Jack got an invitation to debrief the director and Jeff Yanko; both were still fuming about not being invited to the White House. The director in particular saw it as a significant snub. The debrief was only meant to take an hour, but Jack thought it would be much shorter than that since there was not much to follow up on from the meeting with the president.

When the meeting time came, Jack made his way upstairs to the director's office and checked in with the receptionist, who told him to take a seat and wait. Jack always felt that people in power wanted people to wait for a while with meetings like this to show them that they were firmly in control.

After a few minutes, they were ready to see him, and he made his way to the director's office. Jeff Yanko was already in there, talking to the director.

The director looked up and saw Jack, beckoning him to come in. He took a seat at the conference table next to them.

The director started, "Jack, don't read too much into this meeting — it's the standard protocol. We just need to know if we need to follow up on anything, from an agency standpoint."

Jack smiled nervously, "The meeting was pretty straightforward. We essentially went through the prepared slide deck, and they asked very few questions."

He paused before continuing. "They mostly just wanted clarification on some charts or figures in our presentation. I also recorded their questions in my written follow-up memo they sent to your office this morning."

"So, what do you think their overall impression was with the project?" the director asked.

"They were impressed with it, plus the progress we've made so far. They're also eager to know when we'll reach full production and expand to other capabilities with the lab."

"Excellent work, Jack," the director beamed. "I'm so pleased the president's office has a favorable impression of the project, as well as our agency right now. It's super helpful to have their support, particularly as budget cycles are approaching."

"Well, it's a team effort," Jack replied. "I appreciate the support from Jeff and my team, who pulled all the presentation material together. I was just the messenger," he added humbly.

The director replied, "Well, I know we had scheduled this meeting for an hour, but based on the memo you submitted and hearing it from you, I think we have all we need for now. I'll give you some time back in your day. Thanks again for all your hard work on this."

Jack returned to his office while Yanko stayed back, presumably to continue his discussion with the director.

• • • •

"He doesn't know what's going on?" the director said to Yanko after Jack had left.

"Nothing. He's such a Boy Scout," Yanko replied, happy to put this behind him and continue working on fast track.

• • • •

Soon after meeting with the director and Yanko, Jack reached out to Frank and scheduled a time for him to come to his office to bring him up to speed. A few minutes before they were supposed to meet, Jack heard a knock on his door and looked up to see Frank standing at the entrance.

"Good to see you, Frank; thanks for coming by," Jack began. "Come on in and make yourself comfortable."

Frank shut the door and pulled up a chair in front of Jack's desk, immediately saying, "I'm eager to hear everything that's been going on over the past few days."

Jack laughed, "Well, I'm glad to have all that over. The meeting at the president's office was certainly stressful, but the briefing itself was straightforward with very few questions."

"I'm surprised they didn't hit you with a lot of detailed questions," Frank replied. "On the other hand, they probably don't know enough about the technology to ask the right ones."

"My thoughts exactly," Jack smiled. "I'm not sure they knew what they were looking for, just wanting a sense of the project's overall health I suspect."

"So, there were no real surprises during the briefing?"

Jack paused for a moment. "No, the only thing out of the ordinary is President Witte kept me behind after. He wanted to know if I had anything else to add, without all the extra company in the room."

"Oh?" said Frank with some excitement in his voice. "How did you reply to that?"

Jack quickly spoke, "Don't worry, I didn't tell him anything — though I thought about it for a moment. To me, it seemed he was fishing for information, but he didn't have anything to go on. I decided to leave things as they are and let this play out a bit."

He pressed on. "I also got the same type of response from the director and Yanko when I spoke with them. I assured them everything was normal and nothing was out of the ordinary. They seemed to take it hook, line, and sinker."

Frank grinned, "I'm guessing you're relieved by the outcome of the meetings and having both of them in your rearview mirror?"

"Exactly. I just needed to get through both events with no stumbles. I'm not exactly sure what to do next, but I knew neither could help us with what we're dealing with."

Frank got up out of his chair before saying, "I'm happy things went well. I'm sorry, I have to run — I need to get to another meeting and still have a little prep work to do. Thanks again for the update. I appreciate you sharing all this with me."

"Of course. Unfortunately, we are in this together!"

Frank left Jack to his emails. He scanned them, feeling a moment of relief, but he did not know what his next steps were for dealing with this situation. For now, he would take a bit of the peace and move on with the rest of his day.

• • • •

Jack and Lucy finished dinner that evening and relaxed in their family room. It was a rare evening when they had time to sit down and watch some TV or a movie. In this case, however, they were both exhausted and just wanted to sit and chat for a while.

"How are you doing this evening?" Jack opened the conversation. "How's everyone handling things at the senator's office?"

"I'm just drained and pretty raw right now," Lucy replied.

Jack smiled and reached out to grasp her hand. "You've been through a lot these last few weeks; I completely understand how painful all this must be."

"I just realized today that I really couldn't continue in the senator's office. I need to get away from it all." Lucy's voice quivered.

"I'm not surprised," Jack nodded. "I think it's the best thing for you to move on to something else. I think it will give you some closure."

Lucy sighed. "I can't wait to get back home to Ohio and get a fresh start."

"I've been thinking the same thing. I feel trapped with all this going on. Maybe we can finally put some distance between ourselves and the situation."

Lucy nodded, her eyes glistening. Jack headed into the kitchen to pour them each a glass of wine, and they continued to talk well into the evening. Both felt relieved they were on the same page and could start moving forward with a different chapter of their lives, though Jack knew the situation would not simply go away. He would be dealing with this for months to come.

Chapter 13 The Move to Ohio

A week or so after Jack and Lucy had their serious talk about moving to Ohio, they began to work on a plan. Since Lucy was having great difficulty at work, they decided she would leave her job first and stay with relatives in Ohio. She would use this time to look for an apartment she and Jack could move into once Jack had transitioned out of the agency.

Meanwhile, Jack would start looking for a job while still employed at the agency. Once he found a suitable one, he could put their condo on the market and make moving arrangements to join Lucy. Neither had any idea what the job market was like in the Dayton area, but they hoped they could find something reasonable to match their career aspirations.

It didn't take Lucy and Jack long to solidify the details of their plan and start the process of moving. Though still uncertain about their future, Jack felt good coming to a joint decision they were both comfortable with.

• • • •

Soon after they had decided to move, Lucy put in her two-week notice at the senator's office. She knew this was the right move, but it was still an emotional experience. She had worked so hard to get her dream job in the nation's capital, and now she was giving up on it. The only thing that kept her moving forward was that she was moving back home — close to her family.

She used this time to say goodbye to the many friends she had made while working for the senator. They were very supportive and understood what she was going through. She felt blessed to have so many good friends who had many kind things to say to her and help cheer her up.

Lucy's first step in transitioning out of the office was to schedule meetings with some of the key personnel to bring them up to speed. Most people she met with were very appreciative of her time and effort during this challenging period.

About a week before her final day, Lucy discovered the staff was planning her a goodbye party on her last day. She was grateful and knew that they meant well, but it would be challenging to go. It would bring up so many painful memories of the senator and her time working there.

The staff had arranged the party around noon, using their lunch hour, and had food catered in. Lucy made her final rounds, talking to people she had not yet said goodbye to. She feared her emotions would run away with her at the party but managed to maintain her composure.

Near the end of the party, one of her coworkers made a brief speech about Lucy's time in the service office, complimenting her valuable contributions. Soon after, it was Lucy's turn to speak. She was so overcome by emotion that she could only offer a quick, sincere thanks to everyone there.

. . . .

The Saturday after her last day at the senator's office, Lucy began packing up some of her things to move to Ohio. She planned on just taking some clothing and other items to keep her going until Jack joined her later with the rest of their belongings.

She would head out the following day, looking forward to spending some time with her family since she had not seen much of them after moving to Washington DC. Luckily, her parents still had a reasonably large house with plenty of room for her.

Once settled in with her parents, Lucy started looking for a new place to live for her and Jack. One pleasant surprise was that finding an apartment in the Dayton area was a breeze compared Washington DC. Within a week or so, she found a suitable place and signed a lease. She had shown Jack pictures, and he seemed to like it. It had everything they needed, including some nearby trails that were great for running. Jack was excited about that.

Lucy moved in quickly and shopped for a few things to brighten up the place until Jack arrived. She could now concentrate on looking for a job and use the opportunity for a little downtime.

Before leaving the senator's office, many of the staff told Lucy they would reach out to their contacts to see if they could help her find a job. It was a nice gesture, but she wondered if any would actually follow through.

Once again, Lucy had underestimated her former teammates' work ethic and resolve. Several had met their promises and forwarded Lucy's résumé to their contacts. Soon after moving into the new apartment, Lucy's phone started chirping from potential employers.

After a few phone interviews, Lucy met a couple of people on-site for a second. The most promising of these was an administrative position at the University of Dayton, supporting the University president. Lucy was surprised how quickly the interviews went, and after the third round with the University president himself, she managed to land the job.

It would still be a couple more weeks before Lucy could start her new job, but she was happy to begin a new chapter of her life. Hopefully, this would take her mind off all the trauma she had been through during the last few months.

• • • •

The morning after Jack and Lucy had decided to leave Washington DC, Jack ran into Frank in the coffee room. It was fortunate timing because Jack wanted to tell Frank what was going on about the move.

Jack opened up with, "Good morning Frank, how are things going for you today?"

"Not too bad so far, but it's still early," Frank replied.

Jack laughed, "I know that too well; I never make predictions this early in the morning. Hey, do you have a second to stop by my office so I can bring you up to speed on something?"

"Yes, I have time right now if you only need a few minutes," Frank nodded.

Jack finished pouring his coffee. "That would be great. It won't take long — we just need a bit of privacy."

Once at Jack's office and the door was shut, Jack began. "I'm guessing you won't be surprised by this, but Lucy and I have decided to move back to Ohio. We talked last night, and she just can't continue with her work in the senator's office after all that's happened."

Frank sipped his coffee and replied, "I'm not surprised by this at all. Of course, I'm sorry to see both of you go, but I completely understand the motivation."

"I'm guessing your next question will be if I will continue working on surveilling the quantum computing lab. If you're willing to provide me the data, then I feel compelled to keep working on this since the consequences might be so dire," Jack replied.

Frank quickly spoke, "I hoped you would say that. I will, of course, continue to support us. I know this was dumped in both our laps, but if we don't continue the work, the situation will get out of control. I shudder to think of the consequences this might have in the long term."

Jack nodded. "I agree with you entirely. I'll also reach out to Jeffers today and let him know what's going on. As far as I'm concerned, nothing changes with the project; I'll just be in a different place."

"Jack," Frank began, "I really hope this works out well for you, and I wish you and Lucy the best of luck. If there's anything I can help with, let me know. I still have contacts in the Dayton area from when I went to school there."

Jack appreciated Frank's support and knew they would continue to work well with each other. Despite Jack on his way out of the agency, he still had a packed schedule, so they had to quickly wrap up their discussion and move on to the day's activities.

Strangely, Jack felt relieved now that he had told Frank of his plans to relocate. It wasn't as though he was hiding anything from anyone, but his plans felt more real now that he had told someone else about them.

• • • •

As Lucy settled into the new apartment and her role at the university in Dayton, Jack began a job search in earnest and started applying to several positions he found online. He hoped the search wouldn't take too long since he was lonely living by himself in DC. He also continued to feel the pressure of his current situation at the agency.

In Jack's favor, many high-tech companies operated in the Dayton area, supporting research and development contracts from Wright-Patterson Air Force Base. Jack was highly qualified in any computer science area and had excellent project management skills he could transfer to most roles.

Jeffers knew Jack was looking for a new job and had extensive contacts with his air force buddies, some of who worked at the base. He had sent an email to Jack, telling him the Air Force Institute of Technology was looking for a full-time computer science professor. Jeffers forwarded him a link to the job description, telling him that he knew the college dean.

Fortunately for Jack, the timing on this position was just right. It was now summertime, and the Air Force Institute of Technology needed someone to start quickly for the fall semester. The idea of teaching really appealed to him; it would allow the opportunity to go back to basic research and getting more into the technical side of things. It would also get Jack out of the political management he had entangled himself in with his current job at the agency.

After a couple of rounds of interviews, Jack landed the position and notified the agency, talking to Jeff Yanko about his transition out of the quantum computing lab's management job. Of course, Yanko was supportive of Jack's move and told him he understood the difficult time Lucy was having, happy to be rid of his subordinate. He thought that moving back home was a good move for both of them, but Jack knew it meant him leaving was one less problem Yanko had to deal with, and he could now handpick someone to replace Jack.

The only thing left to do now was for Jack to sell their condo in Alexandria and arrange a mover to pack up their things. Fortunately for Jack and Lucy, the market was red hot in Alexandria, so their condo was only up for sale for a couple of weeks, and they got even more than their asking price. Jack arranged a quick closing date so he could move to Ohio right away, thankful this whole transition happened reasonably quickly.

Jack was also happy with the timing of him starting at AFIT. In the mid-summer, he would arrive in time to give himself adequate preparation for the courses the university scheduled him to teach, beginning at the end of August.

After closing on the condo and the movers had loaded everything into the truck, Jack got in his BMW and drove to Ohio to begin his new career. Moving out of DC would not make the situation with the quantum lab disappear, though putting distance between himself and the agency would take some of the pressure off.

· · · ·

When Jack first told Jeffers he was leaving the agency and moving back to Ohio with Lucy, it started the wheels turning for Jeffers. He had become increasingly uncomfortable with his position in the agency and began to feel more and more like an outsider every day. The environment was toxic, and he no longer trusted the management. He was also especially suspicious of both the agency director and Jeff Yanko. The data Jeffers had seen coming out of the quantum lab had shocked him; he knew fraud was happening on a massive scale. This made the decision easy for Jeffers to reach out to some of his old contacts within the air force.

Since Jeffers was a liaison officer only temporarily appointed at the agency, it would be easy for him to transition out. He would just need to find one of his contacts with a higher priority assignment and use the air force brass as leverage to leave.

One of Jeffers's contacts was the technical director at the National Air and Space Intelligence Center. Jeffers reached out and told him about his situation. Fortunately for Jeffers, his contact at NASIC was looking for someone to help with their technology assessment programs. This agency's mission was to look at foreign technology and assess the United States' military threat.

Jeffers interviewed with the agency and landed the job within a reasonable amount of time. Coincidentally, Jeffers would start his new position just a couple of weeks after Jack would arrive at Wright-Patterson. In the back of his mind, Jeffers knew they would continue their work of surveilling the quantum computing lab. They needed to find a way to slow or stop whoever was stealing agency resources. Jeffers did not look forward to continuing with the project, but he knew it would be necessary since there was no one else to stop it.

THE RISE OF THE DEEP STATE

Chapter 14 The Presidential Election

President Witte was in good shape for his reelection. Things were going well with the economy and the stock market, his approval ratings remained strong, and he seemed confident in his reelection bid.

The President had a substantial lead over the democratic candidate and seemed to be almost a sure thing for reelection. This lead was not surprising since most of his first term was pretty smooth, and the country's overall satisfaction remained high.

It also helped that things were relatively quiet on the foreign-policy front. US's traditional enemies had been silent for a sustained period, and President Witte had managed to pull the country out of most foreign entanglements they had trapped themselves in for years.

President Witte ran on a more central theme, though he was sometimes labeled as a conservative republican. He had promised to bring more stability to the government following some very turbulent years before his election. At the current time, he was enjoying an all-time high in popularity.

The president also had a very likable personality, outgoing with a love for sports and being outside. He regularly attended high-profile sporting events and genuinely enjoyed being a part of them. His favorite was college football, regularly attending games and using it to enhance his image as an average guy, and he was a big Ohio State Buckeyes fan since he was an alumnus.

In early winter, most people assumed President Witte had complete control of the election, and the democratic candidate would not be able to present much of a challenge.

• • • •

Early spring, a third-party candidate entered the race as an independent — Michael Graham, a conservative democrat from Minnesota. He started building a platform as an alternative to the two major parties. Despite being in the Senate for quite some time, Graham labeled himself as an outsider and wanted to use his election to shake things up in Washington DC.

Graham was barely statistically significant in the polls — almost nonexistent and received very little press — when he had entered the race. There was no indication he could get major backers or funding and really make a noteworthy run against the two major parties.

Soon after announcing his candidacy, the stock market began to waiver, and rough weeks of trading and high volatility were seen. President Witte made several remarks at a press conference, stating that these were just short-term aberrations and nothing to be concerned about. However, the more he talked about it, the worse things seemed to get.

Eventually, after significant market turmoil, the job market began to turn too. What had been an amazingly steady period of low unemployment in the United States suddenly changed, and the economy started to shift.

Though new to the race, Graham used this as an opportunity to chip away at the administration. His numbers began to rise slightly, and he started getting some attention from the traditional press. The rise wasn't too significant, and he still didn't present a threat to either of the traditional party candidates, but he was starting to build a little bit of momentum.

As the economy began to run into some serious issues, a scandalous incident from the Democratic Party candidate's past was revealed. Press had a feeding frenzy, and the scandal began to derail his campaign. The democratic candidate had to spend all his resources defending his past and trying to clean up his reputation rather than laying out new policies that would challenge President Witte.

This represented somewhat of a perfect storm against President Witte, as many democratic supporters started to change their allegiance and move toward the independent candidate, Michael Graham.

At this point, President Witte still had a significant lead over the independent candidate — a remote challenge with less than ten percent polling numbers. However, it was a little alarming how quickly Graham had moved from virtually nothing to a minor percentage. Still, the president seemed to remain firmly in control of the race, with little concern in his campaign.

• • • •

As the campaign entered summer, economic turmoil increased. The market saw unprecedented volatility, with huge spikes and valleys causing it to throttle itself. Profit and risk-taking continue to drive.

Long-term investors begin dumping assets to protect themselves and put things in safer investment vehicles, such as cash and long-term, low-risk mutual funds. What had started as just a couple of rough training sessions had now accelerated into some truly wild up and down sessions with historical highs and lows.

It seemed uncanny that every time President Witte made a move to stabilize things, everything just exponentially worsened. Timing made things truly exasperating. It was almost as though the economy was listening to him, pushing back every time he wanted to move forward.

This was some of the most unusual activity Witte's team had ever dealt with. They met in near-crisis mode on an almost daily basis to figure out the next step in stabilizing the economy, solely fixated on the market's instability and rising unemployment numbers.

Because of this, Michael Graham enjoyed a rapid and steady increase in his polling numbers. He had risen well past the democratic challenger, who was beginning to disappear into obscurity. His advertising also increased as he picked up some key endorsements and some much-needed funding for his campaign. His numbers were starting to make some of Witte's campaign team nervous.

Meanwhile, Witte's team thought that the upcoming republican convention would give them a great stage to lay out all the successes they'd had over the last four years and try to downplay this most recent instability. The convention took place over the summer with a well-orchestrated message, banking it would give Witte a significant bounce and leave the independent candidate firmly in the rearview mirror.

After the convention had concluded, however, much of the country had no interest in the republican convention. They were more interested in the state of the economy and the stock market. Many people were now beginning to lose their jobs and depend on unemployment benefits, and things were starting to turn from just a short-term skid to the point where the country was now deeply concerned about the future. President Witte's numbers continued to erode.

. . . .

Now the election had moved into fall, both campaigns ramped up for the November election. Michael Graham had moved within fifteen points of the current president, and the democratic candidate had completely fallen off.

With the state of the campaign now in jeopardy, President Witte called an emergency meeting with his senior staff to strategize their next move. This particular gathering was small, held in the Oval Office with Witte's campaign manager, some of the senior campaign staff, and his chief of staff.

The meeting started off with the campaign manager presenting a series of charts showing public sentiment on various public policy issues. Most of the meeting concentrated on the stock market's instability and rising unemployment numbers. The team desperately tried to make sense of these numbers and the extreme volatility they were seeing.

Near the end of the meeting, the president spoke. "I just don't get it. It seems like every move we make is an extreme blunder. It's almost like somebody has designed something that counteracts whatever policy we put in place, pushing the economy or market in the wrong direction."

He continued. "I know it sounds crazy, but it almost feels like somebody is gaming the system on a massive scale."

"I feel the same way, Mr. President," his chief of staff replied. "But at this point, we need to concentrate our resources. I've put something in action before the election to bolster our numbers."

"I agree; I'm just venting a little," the president sighed. "This has been incredibly frustrating — not just for me, but for all the country. Do you have something specific in mind?"

The chief of staff was ready with an answer. "Yes — the team has put together an unprecedented plan that should put some stability back in the market and allow the economy to get back on its rails."

President Witte was silent for a few seconds, then replied, "All right, give me the write-up on the plan. I'll review it this evening and see if it's something I would like to move forward with. You will have my answer in the morning."

Witte took the papers from his chief of staff and returned to the White House residence to review them and make his final decision. The meeting, filled with tension, ended fairly abruptly. The Witte team *knew* they were in trouble, and this might be their last hope.

The president took his time to carefully review the proposal. It seemed like a sane plan on the surface, but it did put some trading restrictions on the stock market. Many republicans would cringe at the idea of restricting free trades and markets, but it was a risk he needed to take. It might mean alienating some people from his own party, the market, and the country, but they desperately needed some stability from the turmoil.

Witte ultimately decided to approve the proposal and decided to roll it out over the next few weeks, so the timing would coincide with the final push before the election. He gambled that this would give him the final push he needed to get him over the top.

. . . .

The Graham campaign used the latest instability in the stock market to hone his message and promise to restore order. Public sentiment had shifted well past the support they had shown for President Witte earlier in the year as many companies continued to lay off large numbers of employees. The market's unprecedented volatility also influenced major corporations' significant investments from getting underway, some stopping entirely.

The first couple of days after President Witte announced his major stimulus and controls package for the stock market, things seemed promising. But on the third day, the market took an unprecedented tumble, and Witte's controls proved to be ineffective. Graham seized an opportunity to blast the president on his foolhardy plan. Not only did Witte not have positive results, but they actually caused more harm than good in many cases.

The other strange phenomenon was Graham picking up huge numbers on social media, and his campaign seemed particularly adept at generating positive sentiment. This also tied into last-minute fundraising — also particularly positive for his campaign, while they raised record amounts of money and picked up key endorsements at the last minute. Graham's team poured all this money into mass media market campaigns, ruthlessly pounding the message home about the instability of Witte's economic plan.

Both the republican and democratic parties were completely befuddled, with no idea about what had just hit them. There had never before been a third-party candidate who had posed a viable threat to the two-party system, upending their dominance on the country.

• • • •

By late October, it was clear this was a two-horse race between President Witte and Michael Graham. The democratic party had fallen so far off that no one was even talking about the possibility of them winning.

Of course, the press had picked up on this story, changing their interpretation of the polling numbers to the extent that the public lost all confidence in it. The press also tried to present opinions on what was causing the independent candidate's unprecedented rise, but the public wasn't listening.

Graham seized this opportunity to unleash a complete media blitz designed to overwhelm the president and his campaign. The plan was unrelenting and attacked President Witte with incredible precision and timing. Every time the market slipped following President Witte's address, the Graham campaign would jump and make the most of the opportunity. It seemed to be working, and he was poised to take the campaign lead, though the polling numbers seemed unreliable, and the press hadn't confirmed it.

The only person on the Witte campaign who remained optimistic was the president himself. He had been in politics a long time and had an uncanny way of pulling out campaigns at the last minute. He thought this one would be no different. In the back of his mind, however, President Witte knew he was in for the political fight of his life.

Chapter 15 The Beginning of the Resistance

Jack finally joined his wife about six weeks after she left for Ohio. Lucy was happy to be out of the political environment and working at the university as the president's executive assistant. She was fortunate to find such an excellent job in a short amount of time.

It would be three or four weeks before the fall semester would start. Jack had some time to settle in before reporting to his job at AFIT, where he would work on setting up his courses and become familiar with the university's policies and procedures.

Given how quickly they had to make this transition and move out of Washington DC, Jack and Lucy had both ended up with excellent jobs, their connections in DC helping them.

• • • •

Frank called a couple of weeks after Jack moved to Ohio, saying that he wanted to visit to see how things were going. As was their typical exchange, they arranged to play a round of golf while Frank was in town. They both loved the sport but never had enough time to play, let alone together. With everything going on the last couple of months, Jack was looking forward to meeting up.

They went to Beavercreek Ohio Golf Club, just a few minutes from Jack's apartment. It was a quality venue despite being a public course, and both Frank and Jack looked forward to playing.

Since it was midmorning on a Monday, hardly anyone was at the course. The starter allowed just the two of them to go out on their own, and they could go as fast or slow as they wanted. After some small talk a few holes into the round, their conversation turned to the inevitable — the quantum computing lab and its log files and reports.

"Jack," Frank began. "I know how much you wanted to play golf today, but I need to bring you up to date on what I'm finding in the analysis reports."

A strained look on his face, Jack replied, "Yeah, I guess we can't put it off any longer — we may as well get down to business."

Frank stopped the golf cart just short of the next tee. "There certainly has been a lot of activity at the lab these last few weeks. I'm starting to piece together some jobs that are running via the reporting you put in place."

"Yeah," Jack replied as he left the cart to grab his driver. "I could tell the volume was picking up from the snippets of the reports you put in my encrypted folder, but I couldn't quite tell what type of jobs were running."

Frank explained, "From what I'm seeing, Jack, it looks like two types of jobs are running. The first one appears to be some market analysis program looking at specific cause-and-effect relationships. The second job seems to focus on social sentiment and charting how effective a particular advertising campaign is working."

Jack quickly replied, "Frank, are you thinking what I'm thinking? They're using these jobs to manipulate the election!"

"Not only do I think that, but I believe they're actually very successful with it," Frank solemnly replied. "If you look at the job timings in relation to the poll numbers, I think you'll see a one-to-one correlation."

"I've had suspicions about this from the beginning," Jack nodded, equally grim. "They're using the lab as part of an elaborate scheme to steal the presidential election."

Frank thought for a moment. "I can give you more details after the next round of reports. I'll put them in the encrypted folder. You can also leave your detailed notes in there, and we can safely review them online without being overheard on the phone."

"That's fantastic," Jack replied. "I'm eager to take a look at it, but I'm afraid of what I might find."

Jack sighed and continued, "Well, there's no use ruining a good round of golf talking about this any further. It looks like we have a plan of action to move forward. I'll bring Jeffers up to date with what you found. I have no idea what the next steps are, but I'm sure we can figure out a plan between the three of us."

"All right, that's enough about business. Let's get down to some serious golf!"

With their brief conversation over, Jack and Frank could play the rest of the round without distractions, blowing off a little steam and what was to come next in their minds.

. . . .

A few days after golf, Jack called Jeffers to set up a lunch meeting. Jeffers had accepted a job at Wright-Patterson Air Force Base, where Jack was working, and had moved out several weeks before Jack left the agency.

It was more than just a bit of good luck that Jeffers had landed a job at Wright-Patterson; he had pulled in some favors he had built up over the years while in the special forces and knew about the serious nature of what Jack and Frank had stumbled upon. He had vowed to stick with it and thought his best chance of success was being transferred from the agency, so he could operate at a safe distance with Jack.

Jeffers answered the phone with, "Hey, Jack, I hope you're calling to tell me you're in town and ready to meet up with me somewhere!"

Jack laughed, "You must be a clairvoyant because that's exactly what this call is. What do you think about getting together for lunch in the next couple of days?"

"That's fantastic, you just name the time and place, and I will clear my calendar."

Jack quickly checked his schedule and confirmed a meeting a couple of days away at a restaurant just outside the base, Milano's in Beavercreek. It was one of Jack's favorite places to go while in college at Wright State, working on his Ph.D.

Jeffers had already grabbed a table and was waiting on Jack when he arrived. Jack quickly spotted Jeffers and made his way to the table, reaching out a hand to shake and saying, "I can't tell you how good it is to see you again, old friend."

"Great to see you too, but watch who you're calling old!" Jeffers joked.

They spent some time catching up. There was a nervous energy about the conversation as they were both eager to talk about what was going on in the quantum computer lab.

Jack finally broke the ice. "I guess you're dying to hear what's going on with the lab and what I've heard from Frank?"

"Yes, I think about it all the time," Jeffers quickly replied. "What did you find out? I'm hoping for the best, but I also fear the worst and that we'll have to continue dealing with it."

Jack finished a long drink from his ice tea. "Well, you won't be disappointed; a lot *is* going on there. I won't be able to bring you completely up to date over lunch. I played golf with Frank just a few days ago; he sent me some reports."

"I was afraid you would say that," Jeffers moaned. "I hoped this whole thing was some mistake, and it would just go away."

With a twisted look on his face and a small sigh, Jack replied, "I will add you in on the credentials, so you have access to the drop folder location. Then you can start reviewing the data for yourself and make your own conclusions. That's assuming you still want to be involved?"

Without thinking, Jeffers answered, "Of course I want to be involved — I've come this far. I need to see what's going on here and what people are trying to do with such advanced technology."

"From a super high level," Jack pressed on, "it looks like they're using the lab to run advanced simulations to align with certain precise strategies around stock market manipulation and an aggressive public sentiment campaign."

Not missing a beat, Jeffers chimed in, "I assume they're doing this on a massive scale in conjunction with the election? It explains the third-party candidate's unprecedented rising popularity."

Jack smiled. "I guess I'm not the only one who had this suspicion from the beginning."

"So, do you have any idea how we should proceed?"

Paused for a moment, Jack shared his idea. "The best I have is to set up a secure video conference meeting with Frank to see if we can come up with a plan to move forward. Send me your availability over the next couple of days, and I'll set it up."

"I'll do it as soon as I get back to my office," Jeffers replied.

· · · ·

Soon after lunch, Jack set up a secure meeting with Frank and Jeffers. He desperately tried to think of the next step to get the team moving forward. The only thing he could think of was to reach out for some help from someone with a lot more experience than him in these matters.

That would be tricky because this project was sensitive and Jack was uncertain of the administration's loyalty within the agency. Racking his brain to think of whom to contact, only one name continually came to mind: Woody Lane. He'd to help Jack on many occasions when he was Washington's CIA station chief. The more Jack thought about it, the more sense it made to reach out to Woody for help. He would, undoubtedly, be the right guy for the job.

At their meeting, Jeffers began by saying, "All right, Jack, I seem to have a grasp of what's going on, but my big question is, where do we go next?"

"I've been thinking about that a lot, and I don't have a solid answer," Jack replied. "I think we need to reach out, as a group, to someone else to get some help."

Both Frank and Jeffers agreed this was a necessary step. They were, of course, concerned about who that person would be.

Jack eased them by telling them about his plans to bring Woody Lane in.

"That's a terrific idea," Frank quickly jumped in. "He's just the person who can get us going."

Jeffers eagerly nodded in agreement.

"I'm glad you both agree because I didn't have anybody else in mind we could go to," Jack confessed.

With their next step to move the group forward, Jack planned to call Woody to see how receptive he was in helping them.

* * * *

After talking to Frank and Jeffers, Jack reached out to the Washington CIA station chief. Woodrow Lane was a lifelong CIA employee with deep roots in the agency, allowing him to operate at levels very few employees could. Everyone called him Woody, which seemed to have a more friendly tone to it. Make no mistake, although he was a pleasant guy on the surface, this was one man no one would ever want to cross. Once they got on his 'unpleasant' side, they would never come back.

Woody agreed on a time when Jack could call him. Jack had been careful to find a quiet, secure place to have their confidential conversation. Jack dialed the number and waited for Woody to answer.

After just a few rings, Woody picked up the phone. "Hello, Jack, it's good to hear from you. We've not talked in a very long time."

"It's good to hear from you too," Jack replied. "I've had minimal contact with people inside since I left the agency a couple of months ago."

Woody laughed, "I'm envious — you must sleep much better at night."

"I think you might be right about that; I never really thought about it that way."

"Well, I guess this is probably not a social call, but I'd like to hear it from you first," Woody stated.

Jack sighed, "I'm sure you probably could guess what's going on, but I needed to talk to you to see if there's some way you might help. There have been some strange computations happening in the quantum lab. I've been tracking these for some time now. I'm afraid the size and scope of the operations are truly frightening and have mind-blowing implications."

Woody paused for a moment before responding. "I'm not surprised at what you're saying. I've heard some chatter about the quantum lab and the possibility that outside influences are using it for highly unusual purposes."

"I'm almost glad you've heard something about it, but I'm also frightened at the possibilities of what might really be going on."

Woody quickly replied, "Jack, first off, you don't need to sell me on getting involved — I didn't get into this job for the money or retirement benefits. You can count on me to help you however I can. I'm pretty certain there's some evil work going on with the lab. I also think the level of people involved will require some special handling. I have a lot of experience in these situations."

Jack exhaled, feeling as though someone had lifted an enormous weight off his shoulders. "Just saying thanks is not enough, Woody, but that's all I have at the moment."

"I'm assuming Frank and Jeffers are involved in this too?"

"I guess you know me pretty well," Jack laughed.

"My business is to know what's going on in the agency, so don't be surprised," Woody smiled, then added, "I've got to run, Jack. I'll be in touch with you soon, and we can work out a game plan for this. I realize how sensitive it is, so don't worry about that. I appreciate you reaching out to me. If we find out what's really going on here matches up with what I am guessing it is, the entire country could be at substantial risk."

"I really think it is, Woody. I will work to get you the data we've been collecting to get you started. Great talking with you."

While it relieved Jack to get some more help, he was still worried about where this all might lead and the enormous risks involved.

• • • •

After a busy day, Jack and Lucy settled down to watch the election returns. Earlier that evening, the election seemed to be a toss-up; however, as the day continued, it was clear that Michael Graham was having a steamroller effect. The election was no longer in doubt; Michael Graham would have one of the most significant margins of victory of all time.

Neither Jack nor Lucy had anything to say initially. The results didn't surprise them, but they still hoped for a different outcome.

Finally, Lucy broke the silence.

"Jack, I know you would just as soon stay out of this, but you really have to do something. They can't get away with this, and God knows where it will go from here."

Jack replied, a scowl on his face. "I keep hoping this is a bad dream, and all of it will just disappear."

He pressed on. "Yes, I have been working on something, but I'm not exactly sure what direction it will take. I know I had to do something for the sake of our country; I just never dreamed it would be such a nightmare."

Lucy tried her best to summon a smile. "I know how much all this has bothered you, and I'm certain you'll do whatever is right, despite still working through the details. Anything you can do to slow them down will be better than doing nothing."

Jack nodded in agreement. "Thanks for the pep talk. I still have that sinking feeling in my stomach, but after talking to Frank and Jeffers, I think we'll put a team together to move forward. We'll see where this goes."

"For what it's worth, I'm proud of you for trying to make a difference," Lucy smiled.

The end of that conversation marked the true beginning of the resistance. It would have the odds stacked against it, but a small, talented team with great motivation could genuinely make a difference. Jack knew he would need to lead this movement, even though it was the last thing in the world he wanted to do.

· · · ·

After ending his acceptance speech, Michael Graham retired to his hotel room to reflect on his thoughts and how he would move forward with his presidency.

However, his next order of business was to call James Mac to discuss the election results.

Mac picked up after a few rings. "Grammy, this election has exceeded my expectations. Things went just as planned."

"I really can't believe it," Graham replied. "Even with all the hard data we saw, it's just amazing to see it come true."

Mac sighed heavily. "Grammy, you realize this is just the beginning. We will do great things together now that we have control of the country."

"I know, and I can't wait to get started," Graham gushed. "This is a fantastic opportunity for this country to finally get on track."

"Now is the time to activate the people we've had in place for years and get this thing rolling."

"You bet. We're already on it."

Mac's laugh boomed over the line, "Grammy, this is going to be fantastic, like nothing the world has ever seen. Enjoy your victory party tonight; I'll touch base again with you soon."

The United States and the world would never be the same. The era of the Deep State had begun.

Eric Frick

I have worked in software development and IT operations for 30 years as a Software Developer, Software Development Manager, Software Architect, and as an Operations Manager. For the last ten years, I have taught evening courses on various IT related subjects at several local universities in the Columbus Ohio area. In 2015 I founded http://destinlearning.com, and have developed a series of online courses and books that can provide practical information to students on various IT and software development topics.